The Sins with
KIND FACES

Oliver R. Cross

ISBN 978-1-63784-147-1 (paperback)
ISBN 978-1-63784-148-8 (digital)

Hawes & Jenkins Publishing
16427 N Scottsdale Road Suite 410
Scottsdale, AZ 85254
www.hawesjenkins.com

Printed in the United States of America

CHAPTER 1

SAHRA

My name is Paige Striffe, and as of today, I am a full-fledged field agent at SAHRA or Supernatural and Human Relations Association. SAHRA is a secret organization that helps supernatural beings peacefully coexist with humans without humans ever knowing. Kind of like those *Men in Black* movies, minus the aliens, of course. The boring desk agents deal with easy jobs like rogue werewolf packs or a young djinn throwing a hissy fit. Field agents, or yours truly, handle the major cases that deal with the Greek gods and goddesses, or even one of the seven heavenly virtues if you're lucky.

I've worked here ever since my fifteenth birthday, and my grandfather was one of the founders, but he practically raised my twin brother and I after our parents died. They died when we were pretty young, but we still have a lot of good memories with them. When me and my brother, Niko, found out that our parents died on the job, he ran off the first chance he got, and now he is a famous photographer even though he's only twenty. Unlike Niko, I love this job and would never want to work anywhere else. Our grandfather passed away shortly after we turned nineteen, but luckily, by then we had stable jobs and our own places to live. If my parents and grandfather were still here today, I know that they would be so proud of him, and me as well.

The cool morning breeze just added to my good mood as I walked along the sidewalk, headed for work. *Today is the best day ever*, I thought to myself as I walked up the marble steps that lead

1

to the front doors of SAHRA HQ. The front lobby looked like any other office building. Fake plants, some lounge chairs, an attractive young female secretary, and a few big, intimidating security guards. I flashed one of the guards my ID tag and walked right past him to the elevator. After working there for almost six years, I don't think they actually check my ID anymore. After I stepped into the empty elevator, I immediately pushed the button for the forty-sixth floor. The ride was surprisingly quick, but it usually was, thanks to the advancements that allowed the elevator to go all the way up to Olympus and all the way down to hell. As soon as the elevator reached my floor, it chirped, and the doors slid open. I walked over to the cubicle that I shared with a rookie desk worker and set my black denim messenger bag on my desk before I headed to my boss's office. I was definitely way too eager to get my first major job, but I couldn't help it.

As I walked into his office, he looked up from his paperwork and smiled at me. His name is Alex Winters, and I've known him practically my whole life because he worked with my parents. He is a very tall, slender man with dark brown hair and a short beard to match. He used to babysit me and Niko when our grandpa would go away on a long case.

"Good morning, sir. Do you have my first job ready for me?" I asked with maybe a little too much enthusiasm.

Alex laughed a little under his breath and said, "Eager as always, I see, and please stop calling me sir. You know I hate it when you do. It makes me feel old." I just shrugged in response to his request. His grin grew a little deeper as he picked up a very thick stack of folders off his desk. "But for real, the big bosses gave you a pretty massive first case."

I knew from personal experience that every one of those files was an individual's description, and he was holding seven of them. It was hard to believe that all that was one case, and even harder that it was my *first* case.

"That's an awful lot of files, but I didn't make it this far to back out now," I said as I clenched my fist in determination.

"Well, you know I'm rooting for ya, kid, but I don't know what the higher-ups were thinking when they assigned this case to a…

well, a newbie. No offense," he said as his expression faded to one of slight guilt. I felt a twinge of sadness deep in my heart at his words and quickly covered it with a smile.

"None taken. You're just speaking the truth, but I promise you that I will succeed in this case no matter what it takes." I took the stack of files out of his hands a little more forcefully than I had intended to. I took a deep breath and then let it out, sending my faint frustration with it.

He was shocked at first and then he let out a small laugh. "I should've known that once you put your mind to it, there wouldn't be any chance of talking you out of it. Well, that case is dealing with the seven deadly sins. Or more precisely, keeping an eye on them."

I was shocked into silence. *Massive* didn't even begin to cover the seven deadly sins.

"There have been groups of lesser sins rebelling against their high positions. Your job is to stay with them and help maintain the peace. That means keeping the rebels at bay, but it also means keeping the major seven from causing too much trouble. All of them should be waiting for you tonight, at eight o'clock, at the address in the last file. Now get back to your desk, read through those files, and make me proud."

My spirits soared at his last couple words, and I gripped the files a fraction tighter. "I won't let you down, sir," I said as I turned and walked out the door with a slight skip in my step.

"I said stop calling me sir!" he called after me before closing his office door.

CHAPTER 2

Explosive Introductions

I rushed back to my desk with a smile glued to my face. By the time I reached my desk, the rookie, Max, was already there and hard at work. He was an eighteen-year-old boy who just graduated high school. One of his relatives got him the job because otherwise, he wouldn't have known it even existed. Humans aren't supposed to know about this organization unless they work here. He had shaggy blond hair and a surprisingly innocent demeanor for this job, but he hadn't been working here for more than a week.

When I dropped the stack of files on my desk and plopped down in my computer chair, he turned around and gawked at the files with surprise. "Wow! That's a lot of information for one case! They're really piling it on, huh?" he asked me, his voice overflowing with curiosity. He was a really upbeat person for a job where you deal with supernatural beings all day long.

It took everything I had not to laugh at him. It had become a force of habit over the past week for me to tease him, even though he wasn't that much younger than me. "Maybe you'll get cases like this too if you ever become a field agent. I mean, I know you've already finished two cases, which is impressive, but you don't seem very intimidating."

After that, Max turned back around to his paperwork with a sigh and didn't say another word to me.

I finally opened the first file, and the first thing to catch my eye was the picture of a young African American girl. She was wearing a dark purple hoodie that was at least two sizes too big, black-and-white striped leggings, a pair of worn-out work boots, and a silver bracelet. She had long black hair in a braid, two small hoop-shaped piercings in her left eyebrow, and a lollipop stick sticking out of her mouth. I set the picture aside and started reading the information in the file:

Gluttony a.k.a. Grace Sweets. Current human image: a fifteen-year-old African American girl. She is five feet tall, skinny, and loves any kind of food but prefers (ironically) sweets. Her mystical weapon is a chain and sickle. I kept going through the files.

Sloth a.k.a. Simon Fisher. Current human image: an eighteen-year-old American boy with scruffy brown hair, wears sweatshirts and sweatpants most of the time, and is five foot seven. He wears a charm on his sweatshirt all the time. He has a deep love of video games and napping. He also has a strange tendency to fall asleep in any situation, including standing up and in the middle of a conversation. His personality is mostly mellow, but he tends to get kind of grumpy if you wake him up. His mystical weapon is a giant scythe.

Lust a.k.a. Lillian Mavis. Current human image: a thirty-five-year-old American woman with long black hair, a lanky build, and she stands at six foot one. She is often found flirting with anyone around her or smoking. She also wears a black choker that goes with any outfit. She may look like someone out of a model magazine, but has a fiery temper on the rare occasion that she gets rejected. She also spends the majority of her time at bars other than the one she works at. Her mystical weapon is a rapier.

Greed a.k.a. Gabriel Logan. Current human image: a thirty-year-old African American man who dresses in fancy suits and only wears expensive golden jewelry. He has dark brown dreadlocks that come down to his shoulders and stands at six foot six inches. He enjoys committing gang-related crimes but has a good sense of humor if you stay on his good side. He is pretty easy to get along with if his mischievous streak doesn't bother you. His mystical weapons are double handguns.

Pride a.k.a. Preston Scott. Current human image: a twenty-eight-year-old American man who stands at a solid seven feet tall and is around 280 pounds, but it's all muscle. He is completely bald, always wears a bunch of rings, and spends most of his time exercising, but he's not the brightest bulb. He has a huge ego and is altogether not a very fun person to be around, but can be polite on occasion. His mystical weapons are a pair of brass knuckles.

Wrath a.k.a. William Smith. Current human image: a twenty-three-year-old American man with spiky naturally red hair, a decent build, and is six feet tall. He has a gold lip ring and one gold dagger-shaped chain earring in his left ear. He has a hotheaded temper twenty-four seven, likes picking fights with others, and loves destroying things. It takes a lot to get on good terms with this guy, and he usually only shows his good side to his siblings. His mystical weapons are five throwing knives.

Envy a.k.a. Elizabeth Parker. Current human image: a twenty-five-year-old American woman with short blonde hair, which is usually held out of her face with a hairpin, and decent looks. She loves going to the mall as well as getting her hair and nails down several times a week. She is always on the lookout for gossip and spreads it just as much. She is five foot ten and has a sassy attitude, but usually gets irritated if you boast about something you have that she doesn't. She can become obsessive in getting that object or a copy of that object. Her mystical weapon is a metal whip.

There was an extra paper in Envy's file just like Alex had said. The piece of paper had "4382 Mosscreek Road" written in his sloppy handwriting. I slid the piece of paper into my pocket and went through the files a couple more times, attempting to memorize as much as I could about these sins. I knew that working with them would probably be easier if I didn't make them mad from the start. After hours of looking up all the information I could about them in the organization's database, I glanced at the clock on my desk to see that it was seven thirty. *Oh crap*, I thought to myself as I jumped out of my seat and shoved their files into my messenger bag.

Once I got out the front door, I ran down the sidewalk as fast as I could. It was dark outside, but the streets of the city were still very busy with people heading home from work or going out for a party night. I finally turned onto the street, panting from having run the whole way. I slowed down to a walk as I looked around for the address. When I finally spotted the number, I found myself standing outside of a small bar. I thought it was a strange place to meet until I remembered that Lust worked at a bar.

I took a deep breath before I stepped through the front door. Once inside, I realized that the place was nearly empty except for seven people that were undoubtedly the sins. Lillian was cleaning glasses behind the bar while talking with Gabriel, who was drinking shot after shot, and Elizabeth, who was filing her nails. Simon was asleep at one of the tables while Grace happily gorged herself on bar peanuts. Preston was facing off against William in a game of pool.

At first, they didn't seem to notice that I was there. As I was trying to figure out the best way to introduce myself, William looked up from his game, like he could sense that I was there, and saw me. His eyes narrowed in agitated disbelief. "You're the SAHRA agent they sent us? You don't look like you could help a fly," he said in a mocking tone. He looked so irritated at my presence.

Those words stung a little as the others turned to look at me. Then Grace spoke up in my defense, "You don't have to be so mean, William. You of all people should know that looks can be deceiving, spikey."

"What did you just call me? Last time I checked, my hair is perfectly fine just the way it is. As if you have any room to talk. At least I wash mine!" he protested as he marched right up to Grace.

"I never said anything about my hair being better than yours. I just said it was spiky, and I think it looks like you have a red porcupine on your head," she replied around a mouth full of peanuts.

I could practically see the steam coming out of his ears before Lillian intervened. "That's enough out of both of you. She may not look like much, but she is still a SAHRA agent and is here to help us. Besides, if you don't stop yelling, you are going to wake up Simon, and you know he's not exactly pleasant when he's woken up," she said in a firm voice. Then she set the glass down that she was polishing and walked straight up to me. To my surprise, she grasped my right hand, brought it to her lips, and kissed the back of it. "My name is Lillian Mavis, but you can call me Lily if you like, mon cheri."

I felt my face get hot and pulled my hand away. I didn't want to be rude, but I wasn't into girls, especially not one that I had known for less than five minutes.

Gabriel let out an amused laugh at my gesture. "I don't think she likes you very much, Lily."

"I...I meant no offense, Ms. Mavis. It's just...well, you see, I..." I was too bewildered to finish my sentences.

Then she gave me a wide smile. "You don't have to be so formal. Like I said, call me Lily, and I apologize if I made you uncomfortable."

I grinned back at her but was still a little surprised. Her file had said she would get mad if she got rejected, but there was no hint of anger toward my reaction.

"The rest of you, get over here and introduce yourselves," she said after turning back toward the others. She acted kind of like their mother, but I guess that's how it would work if you were supposed to be the oldest of seven.

All the others stopped what they were doing and came over to meet me, except for Simon. who was still sound asleep at his table. Grace was the first one to offer a handshake to me. "My name is Grace Sweets. The sin of Gluttony. Unlike my very rude brother, I believe you'll do just fine in helping us."

I had only just met her, but her words were already inspiring.

Next was Gabriel. "I'm Gabriel Logan. The sin of Greed, and I'm proud of it. As for my little statement earlier, I was just messing with ya. You really can't take anything I say seriously, kid," he said with a smirk that didn't quite reach his eyes. I could already tell that this guy was going to tease me—a lot. I guess that's karma coming back to get me for teasing Max.

When Preston walked up to me, I felt like an ant. I wasn't very muscular, and I was only five foot eight, so he towered over me and was pretty intimidating. Then he grinned at me and playfully smacked me on the shoulder almost hard enough to knock me on my butt. "I'm Preston Scott. The sin of Pride, which tells you everything about me."

Elizabeth eyed me suspiciously and wouldn't shake my hand, but she still introduced herself. "My name is Elizabeth Parker. The sin of Envy. Make sure you don't forget it." She either didn't like me or was already envious of me for some reason.

William still looked at me like I wasn't supposed to be there. I knew that his file said that he was a hothead, but I hadn't done anything to make him mad. "I'm William Smith. The sin of Wrath. Don't bother remembering it. I'm sure you won't stick around long," he grumbled before stalking back over to his pool table.

My concerned expression must have been showing on my face because Lillian placed a reassuring hand on my shoulder. "Don't worry about him, mon cheri. That's just the way he is, but let's move on. The young man asleep on the table over there is Simon Fisher. The sin of Sloth. I'm sure he'll be pleased to meet you when he gets up. Well, I guess that just leaves you. What's your name?"

"My name is Paige Striffe, and as you know, I am a field agent for SAHRA. I swear that I will help you out any way that I can," I replied in the best confident voice that I could muster. After a moment of awkward silence, everyone went back to what they were doing. I wasn't exactly sure how I was supposed to help these people that could probably kick my butt with their pinkie finger, but it was my job nonetheless.

Before anyone else said a word, the window that was only a few feet from me shattered, and I felt something slide past the side of my face before I could cover it. Then I felt something tap the side of my boot and looked down to see a grenade minus its pin on the floor right next to me. Cold terror ran through my veins as I stumbled back in shock. I hadn't known the sins for any more than ten minutes, and I was already going to be blown up.

"Paige, look out!" I heard someone say before I was yanked back into somebody's embrace. We both stumbled back a few more steps before we fell to the floor, their body protectively shielding me from the grenade. Then a loud explosion rang through the bar, and I reflexively clung to the person's clothing and shut my eyes as tightly as I could. A second later, the smoke alarm started blaring and the sprinklers flipped on, drenching us in cold water.

My ears were still ringing when I heard someone faintly calling my name. "Paige? Paige, are you all right?" It took me a second to realize that it was Lily's voice calling out to me, but she wasn't the person on top of me. I groaned and slowly opened my eyes.

My vision was fuzzy, and as I tried to focus on the face in front of me, I heard his voice. "Hey, are you okay?" Sure enough, the person who had shielded me from the blast was William. When I didn't respond, he started shaking my shoulders. "Say something."

"Dude, stop shaking her. You're going to knock her brain loose," said a voice to my right that sounded like Gabriel, but I wasn't quite sure.

My vision was still fuzzy, and my mind was even fuzzier, but I managed a response, "I...I think I hit my head, but I'll be okay... maybe." Hearing my own voice made my head throb, and I winced in pain. I forced my brain to process everything that happened, and it hurt even worse. "What happened? Is everyone okay? We...we should probably leave before..." I rubbed my temple, unable to say anything else through the pain in my head.

"Hey, hey, slow down, sweetie." It was Lily's reassuring voice speaking to me. I felt someone gently place their hand on my shoulder and assumed it was her.

"Lily, she's got a point. We need to get out of here before the cops show up. Human cops wouldn't understand this situation, and besides, the longer we sit here, the wetter we're going to get. Let's get you off the ground," Gabriel said, then reached out, grabbed my hands, and pulled me to my feet. My vision wasn't clear to begin with, but once I was on my feet, everything started spinning. I stumbled a step forward and tripped over my own feet.

Lily grabbed my arm to steady me. "William, I think you gave the poor girl a concussion. She can't even walk straight."

"I'll be okay. I just have to...get my eyes to stop swimming, that's all," I said and could hear the police sirens getting louder through the ringing in my ears.

"Paige, you're going to have to let one of us carry you. You can't walk like that, and we need to leave now."

My mind had gotten so fuzzy I couldn't even tell who was speaking to me. I just groggily nodded before someone hoisted me over their shoulder and everything went black.

CHAPTER 3

Lesser Sins

I felt something soft as my mind started to resurface from the darkness. I could faintly smell garlic, and my headache came rushing back when I opened my eyes due to the bright sun spilling in a nearby window. I was in a luxurious living room, but other than that, I had no idea where I was. I sat up on the couch that I had been asleep on, and a fluffy blue blanket slid off me. Then Grace appeared in the doorway with a relieved smile on her face.

"I'm glad you're awake. I will be right back," she said and left the room. She quickly returned with a steaming coffee mug in her hands. "Here, this is for your headache. Lily said it would help." She handed me the mug and sat down next to me on the couch.

The mug was definitely not filled with coffee, but the liquid smelled kind of like mint leaves and citrus. "Thank you. What is this?"

"It's some kind of herbal mixture. Lily makes it a lot when she has a headache. Me, myself, and I would much rather have a soda or an energy drink, but to each their own I guess," she said before flipping open the pizza box on the coffee table and grabbing a slice.

I had so many questions that I didn't know where to start, and they all just started pouring out at once. "Where am I? What happened last night? Where are the others? Did I—"

"Whoa, whoa, whoa. Slow your roll. You're inside our house for starters. Then Lillian left to deal with the issue at her bar, Simon is asleep in his room, Preston is at the gym, Elizabeth is at a coffee shop down the road, William took a ride around the city on his motorcycle, and Gabriel is dealing with some work business. As for last night, how much do you remember?" she asked, making sure to keep her voice quiet throughout the whole conversation, which I was thankful for.

"Well, I remember the window shattering and the glass going everywhere." I paused there and reached up to run my hand along my cheek. There was a sharp burn, and I could feel a string of dried blood on my face. "Then I saw the grenade, and someone pulled me away, and we fell. I remember the explosion, but everything is pretty fuzzy after that."

"A large piece of glass cut your face, and Gabriel said it would probably leave a scar, but you didn't need stitches. As for your knight in shining armor, that would be William. Deep underneath that cold exterior, he has a good heart, but would never admit that he was really worried when you passed out. You actually scared us all until we got here and Gabriel gave you a thorough examination. He said you had a mild concussion from hitting your head on the floor. And before you ask, yes, Gabriel has medical training. He can be pretty smart when he wants to be," she said while I sipped my drink. It actually didn't taste too bad and eased my headache a little.

As I processed my thoughts, a pang of guilt shot through me. "I'm sorry. I was sent to help keep the peace, and you guys ended up protecting me. I guess I'm not very good at my job." I looked down into my drink as if it would give me the answer as to what to do next.

"I think that is yet to be determined," someone said from the doorway. When I looked up, it was Simon. He had dark circles under his sleepy green eyes, and his brown hair was disheveled. He came over and sat down in the chair across from us before continuing, "I wasn't awake for the introductions, but I'm Simon Fisher. I did a little bit of asking around on the internet and discovered that you have never been on a major case before. I don't know what you expected, but with us being targeted, last night's issues were bound to occur sooner or later."

I was surprised at first, but when I could speak again I didn't know what to say. How had he gotten that information, and how could he be so calm about almost being blown up? Then a thought clicked in my mind. "Was anyone else hurt?"

Grace laughed before answering, "No, we may look like humans, but our bodies are a lot more durable than yours. We haven't lived this long for no reason. That's why William placed himself between you and the grenade. His body could take it, but if you had taken the brunt of that explosion, you could have been severely injured, if not killed. We also heal a lot faster than you if we do get hurt."

We sat there in silence for a few moments while I thought about everything. "Did the person who blew up the bar get away?"

"Yeah, but we know for a fact that it was more than one person and that they are definitely a group of lesser sins. I would say it's not safe for you to be around us, but you crossed that line the minute you took our case, and there's no going back now," Simon said without looking at me. With the type of words that he used, I could tell that he was pretty smart, but his tone suggested that he couldn't care less about what was going on.

Just then I heard someone come through the front door.

"I'm home," Lily said as she walked into the room. "How are you feeling, mon cheri?" she asked and came over to sit down on the other side of me. She placed a cool hand on my forehead and grinned in relief. "Your fever has gone down. That's good. How do you like the tea?"

"It tastes good and helps with the pain. Thank you very much," I said, trying to be sincere. Then another question popped into my head. "This is probably a long shot, but did you guys bring my stuff with you?"

"I'm sorry, mon cheri, your bag was shredded during the explosion. I did find your phone when I went back today, but it was no longer in one piece either." There was genuine sympathy in her voice. They had blown up my files, my phone, and anything else important I had in my bag, great.

"Um, it's all right. There's no need for you to apologize, but can I borrow a phone so I can contact my boss? I'm sure he's in panic mode right now after last night," I asked, setting my mug down on the coffee table.

13

"Here, use mine," Grace said as she pulled her phone out of her sweatshirt pocket and tossed it to me. Then they all got up and left the room to give me some privacy.

I pulled up her contacts and dialed Alex's number. The phone rang three times before he finally picked up. I could tell by his tone that he had been up all night. "Hello? Who is this?"

"Alex, it's Paige. You sound horrible—" I said before he cut me off.

"Paige! Oh my gods! Are you all right? Where are you? What happened?" He was talking so loud that I had to pull the phone away from my ear or I was going to be deaf.

Then I shouted at the phone to get his attention, "Alex! Calm down, I'm okay. Someone tried to blow up the bar shortly after I got there, but I'm staying with the major seven now. I'm sorry I didn't call you sooner. The explosion destroyed my phone." I decided that it would be better to refrain from telling him about the concussion—and the large gash on my face.

"You scared the crap out of me. I was beginning to think that you were dead, but…I'm glad you're all right. I have the feeling that you aren't going to let me take you off this case, so just promise me you'll be careful and check in with me," he said in a firm voice.

"I promise. Thanks for understanding, Alex. I'll talk to you later." After Alex said goodbye, he hung up, and I was left alone in the silence. I sat there for a few more moments before the uneasy silence drove me off the couch and out of the room. I walked down the hall and turned into a room that turned out to be a very spacious kitchen. Lily was sitting at the kitchen table across from Grace. I handed the phone back to Grace. "Thanks."

"Don't mention it. As much as I would love to stay and chat, I have a date to get to. See ya later," she said as she hopped out of her seat and walked to the door. As soon as she opened it, she slammed it shut again. "Never mind, I'm staying right here," she said, quickly marching back into the kitchen. I was completely confused and had no idea what could keep her from going on a date—except food.

"What's wrong, Grace?" Lily asked before I got the chance to.

"Oh, nothing much. There's just a horde of sins and godly monsters standing at our doorstep," she replied in sarcastic irritation.

Lily's jaw dropped in shock, but I could see a hint of fear in her eyes.

Before she could respond, I stood up from my chair. "I'll deal with it." Lily opened her mouth to protest, but I spoke first. "Look, Lily, it's my job. I was sent here to help, and I'm not just going to hide away in your house because of one little setback. Besides, if things go south, I do have combat training. I'm not completely defenseless."

"I don't think you're defenseless, Paige. But your training was against humans or maybe a demigod. We're talking about sins here. They're stronger and faster, not to mention the godly monsters backing them," she said with concern.

"Don't worry, I'll be careful, and you guys will be right inside the house if I need you. I have to at least try and defuse this situation," I said, trying my best to convince her with a smile. After a few moments of hesitation, she slowly nodded. I headed for the door with anticipation building in the pit of my stomach. I stopped just in front of the door, took a deep breath to hide the hesitation on my face, and opened it.

CHAPTER 4

Unscheduled Doctor's Visit

As soon as I opened the door, I was attacked by a roar of protest. There had to have been at least thirty beings surrounding the front of the house, and they all looked completely outraged. I didn't know how else to get their attention, so I yelled at the top of my lungs, "*Be quiet!*" Then the chaos subsided as they all stared at me with suspicion in their eyes. I could feel the pressure of each and every one of their gazes, but it made me stand even straighter than I was before.

"All of you have the right to peacefully protest, but breaking windows and blowing up bars is definitely crossing the line. These people are currently under SAHRA's supervision, so I suggest that you all leave before I have you removed from the premises," I said, my voice holding a surprising note of confidence. A few of them shrank away at the mention of SAHRA, but none of them showed any signs of leaving.

Then a tall skinny woman with dyed red hair came marching right up the porch steps until she was right in front of me. "I'm the sin of Deseat. If you think we don't know that you're on this job alone, then you're wrong, and we aren't leaving until we get what we came for. Whether the major seven hand them over or we pry them from their cold dead fingers is—"

"Over my dead body!" I blurted out without even thinking. What was I thinking—"over my dead body"? Even if this was my first major case, I was too young to die. To my utter disbelief, Deseat

16

just looked at me with a devilish grin on her face that sent a shiver down my spine.

"As you wish," she spit those words like poison, and in the blink of an eye, her fingernails turned into razor sharp claws. She lunged at me, claws aimed for my throat, and I had just enough time to duck before her other hand came racing toward my side. I jumped back, but her claws still ripped through my shirt and jacket. She hadn't injured me, but my jacket was shredded. With the clank of metal, a chain wrapped itself around her arm. Grace was holding the other end of a chain and sickle, keeping Deseat from getting any closer to me.

"Haven't you ever heard of picking on someone your own size?" Her voice was angry, but her expression was excited. I looked back toward the horde when they started shouting again, but Simon was standing in front of me with a giant scythe in his hands.

"This is so troublesome. If you make it out of this alive, you better thank Lily for liking you so much," he said in a voice that sounded like he really didn't want to be bothered.

Then Lily grabbed my arm and pulled me a little farther away from the crowd. "We have to get out of here. They're starting to circle around back," she said, rapidly glancing around for an escape route. As if on cue, I heard the rev of a motorcycle. It came rushing through the crowd of sins and came to a screeching halt right in front of the porch, sending dust flying.

The driver was William, and he did not look pleased with the situation. "Paige, get on. Everyone, meet up at Gabriel's place. We'll figure this out from there," he said and tossed me his helmet. I glanced back at the others. I didn't want to leave them in danger, but I didn't know what I could do. "Hurry up! The others can take care of themselves," he yelled as the horde started surrounding his motorcycle and reaching for him with angry expressions.

I had no other choice but to slip on his helmet and jump on the bike. The helmet was too big, but I couldn't find the sense to care. I just wrapped my arms around his waist and held on as tight as I could, then he revved the engine again and we tore out of the yard. The shouts of the horde died out as we left the house behind us. Everything sped past me and the sound of the whipping wind combined with the engine drowned out all other noises. For a long moment, time seemed to stop. Being pressed up against William's warm back made everything feel almost peaceful.

Due to my adrenaline spike, I couldn't tell how long it took us to come to a stop, but we had stopped in front of a small building at a street corner. It really didn't look like much, but I guess some place conspicuous was a wise decision. I didn't realize I was still gripping William's waist until he spoke up in an irritated tone, "You can let go of me now."

I jolted away from him, slid off the motorcycle seat, and pulled off the helmet. "S…sorry," I said as I felt my face heat up. He climbed off the motorcycle and grabbed the helmet from me to clip it onto his saddlebag.

He walked right up to the door and knocked. After a moment of silence, he started banging on it. "Gabriel, it's me. Open up." Then the door was yanked open, and Gabriel was standing there, tension creeping through his entire body.

"Come on in. Preston and Elizabeth are already here," he said, holding open the door. Me and William walked down a narrow hallway and into a small doctor's office waiting room. The sharp smell of rubbing alcohol made me a little uneasy. There weren't very many seats in the room, but I actually would have preferred to stand. William flopped down in a chair across the room with a long sigh.

CHAPTER 5

Where to Go

We all sat in an awkward silence as we waited for the others to show up. Grace, Simon, and Lillian showed up one by one over the next half an hour. Lillian was the last one to arrive, and as soon as she sat down, we dove into discussion.

"All right, you all know that we aren't going to be able to stay hidden here for long. Maybe a couple days if we're lucky. So we need an alternative," Gabriel said, glancing around at everyone. They all seemed to drift off into thought. Then William looked at me with a mischievous grin.

"Well, a certain someone said she would help us anyway she could, and I'm sure that forcing them to hunt down her house would buy us some time," he said, looking me straight in the eye.

"Oh, no way. It's not that I wouldn't love sharing my place with you guys. It's just…I don't think all eight of us are going to fit in my tiny apartment. But…" I thought hard for a second, then an idea hit me like a ton of bricks. "Can I use the phone?" I asked, pointing toward a telephone attached to the wall. I didn't even wait for an answer as I started dialing a number. Even in the worst situations, there was one person I could count on.

The phone rang a couple times before my brother picked up. "Hello? Who is this?" he asked in his usual business voice that he used with people he didn't know very well.

"It's Paige. Long time no hear, Niko," I said, not able to hide the grin on my face.

19

"Hey, sis. It's good to hear from you. How have you been?" he asked in the playful tone I missed hearing so much.

"I'm all right, but I'm dealing with some work problems right now. Would you mind if me and some...friends crash at your place for a little while?" I hated asking him for things or dragging him into this life after he fought so hard to get out of it, but we didn't have a lot of options.

"Of course. You know you are always welcome here, and any friends of yours are friends of mine. I'm taking a work vacation right now anyway, so I'll be here whenever you decide to stop by," he said.

"Thanks a lot, Niko. I'll owe you one. We'll be there soon," I said before hanging up the phone. When I turned back toward the others, they were looking at me in shock. "We have a place to stay for a little while. It should only take us about a half an hour to get there."

"You mean we're crashing at your boyfriend's place?" Grace said, giving me a knowing look.

"What? No, Niko is my twin brother. I don't have a boyfriend," I said, a little faster than I intended to.

"Wait, Niko is your brother? As in Niko Striffe, the famous photographer? That Niko?" Elizabeth asked in utter disbelief. I was surprised that she actually remembered my last name.

I forced myself to hold back a laugh. "The one and only. He lives outside the city, so it's a great place to lay low, and his house is plenty big enough for all of us. I mean, he lives in a mansion for crying out loud, but if you'd rather stay somewhere else—"

"Nope! At this point, we'll take what we can get. Besides, Elli looks pretty eager to meet your brother," Preston said, jerking a thumb in Elizabeth's direction. Her face was lit up with excitement, and I got the distinct impression that someone had a crush on my brother.

"Well, there's no time like the present. You mind giving us directions to your brother's place?" Grace asked and tossed me her phone.

I pulled up her map icon, punched in Niko's address, and handed it back to her. "Um, who is riding with who?"

"Preston and I can take my car, Grace, Simon, and Elizabeth can ride in Lily's jeep, so I guess you're riding with William. As long as that's okay with you?" Gabriel said with a slight grin. He was embarrassing me, and he knew it.

I felt flustered, but tried to hide it the best I could. "T-that's fine with me." After that, we all left Gabriel's clinic. The others went to their cars. Lily's was parked a few blocks away, and Gabriel's was parked in the parking lot of a store down the street. William grabbed his helmet and tossed it to me. It took me a second to get my grip on it, but at least I didn't drop it.

William swung his leg over the bike and pulled up the kickstand. "Don't just stand there. Get on and try not to squeeze the life out of my waist this time. I swear, it's like you've never ridden a motorcycle before," he said with a short laugh.

His mocking tone made me even more flustered along with a side of irritation. "Actually I never have. I don't really know what I'm doing," I said, fumbling the helmet in my hands.

"Well, then I guess I'll have to teach you, but first you have to put on the helmet and get on the motorcycle," he said and waved me over. I slipped it on and got on behind him the same way he had. "If you plan to keep riding with me, then one of these days we're going to have to get you a helmet that fits, but mine will have to work for now. When you wrap your arms around the driver, link your hands together to keep a better grip." I reluctantly wrapped my arms around him like he said, my heart rate increasing by every movement. Then I felt him grab my hands and guide them up to the bottom of his rib cage, "That way you won't squeeze me to death this time."

I was very glad that I was facing his back because I knew my entire face was beet red. *Come on, self, this is no time to start getting the hots for the sin of wrath!* I thought to myself.

Then Lily's jeep pulled up beside us, and Grace stuck her head out the passenger seat window. "You guys should follow us out of the city. If not for anything else, then to keep William from getting his ten millionth speeding ticket."

"Just shut up and move it," he said, and I could feel him tensing up under my grip. Lily's jeep pulled away, then William revved his engine once and we followed. At some point, Gabriel's sports car pulled up behind us, and we all made our way to the city limits.

CHAPTER 6

Opened Past

As soon as we passed the city limit sign, William pulled around the jeep and stabbed the gas. The tires squealed along the pavement as we popped a wheelie. On instinct, I tightened my grip on him, and although I couldn't hear him, I could feel his body tremble with a chuckle. We pulled way ahead of the others, but they were always in the rearview mirror.

"If you stay hunched behind me the whole time, you're going to miss some pretty awesome views. Just saying," he said loud enough for me to hear him over the engine. After a second of hesitation, I slowly opened my eyes and looked over his shoulder. There were trees surrounding the road as far as the eye could see, and the setting sun had dyed the sky an array of reds and oranges. I was completely awestruck by the beautifully peaceful landscape that was unfolding before us.

Before I knew it, we were turning around to follow the others into my brother's driveway. When we slowed to a stop in front of the mansion, two giant Great Danes came running around the house. I hopped off the bike and handed the helmet to William.

"Duke! Spike! Come here, boys!" I said and kneeled down as they ran over to me. The last time I saw them, they were puppies.

"Awww! Who are these giant babies?" Grace asked as she wrapped her arms around Spike's neck.

I stood up as the others crowded around the dogs. "The black one is Spike, and the gray one is Duke. They are a lot bigger than they were the last time I saw them," I said with a grin. Niko had originally gotten them to be guard dogs, but they're actually big sweethearts.

Then the front doors of the mansion swung open, and Niko came strolling out with open arms. He was always a little taller than me, but it was obvious that he had gotten even taller since the last time I saw him. Now he had to be around six foot three inches, and his eyes were the same emerald green as mine. Our grandpa always told us that our matching light brown hair made him look like a girl, but he grew it out pretty long and was wearing it in a loose ponytail.

I ran straight up to him and wrapped him in a hug. The familiar scent of his cologne was comforting, and I buried my face in his scarf. He squeezed me so tight I thought he was trying to crush me. I couldn't really blame him though. I hadn't seen him since...well, since I had started working at SAHRA. Wow, it definitely hadn't felt like six years.

Niko was the first one to break the embrace, then he grabbed my face and closely examined it. "Oh, Paige, what did you do to your beautiful face?" he asked, his face flooded with concern. He also kept glancing at the tears in my jacket and blouse, like he expected it to start bleeding at any moment.

I gently took his hands off my face and gave him a reassuring smile. "It's just a scratch. I've had way worse." I knew that it probably wouldn't be a good idea to tell him about the whole explosion thing. He could be ridiculously protective.

He didn't press for any more details on the subject, and I was thankful. "So are you going to introduce me to your friends?" he asked as he turned to face the others. I hesitated for a second and looked over to Lillian for help. I didn't know whether to tell him that they were the seven deadly sins, just introduce them by their human names, or both.

To my relief, Lily stepped forward. "If you don't mind me saying, you are just as handsome as your sister is beautiful, bien monsieur," she said, extending her hand to shake his. When he accepted, she continued, "My name is Lillian Mavis, and I just so happen to be the sin of Lust. I hope that doesn't bother you too much."

Niko's jaw practically fell to the ground, and he froze in astonishment. He slowly turned to look me straight in the eye, and stammered out a response, "Paige, honey…You didn't tell me that your friends were of the…supernatural variety."

I really didn't know what to tell him, but I had to say something. "I'm sorry for not telling you before, but I…we couldn't stay in the city, and we didn't have any other place to go. There aren't a lot of options when…when you're being hunted by a horde of godly beings. You were the only one I could trust."

If I didn't think it was completely out of character for him, I would say that Niko looked angry at me. "Wait, you never told me that you were in danger of being killed by godly creatures! How many times have I said that this job is way too risky? I thought hearing about Mom and Dad would have proved that!"

At that instant, I wanted to cry. He had avoided any subject even slightly related to Mom and Dad ever since we found out how they died, and now he was throwing it in my face that the career that I had chosen was what killed them. Every negative emotion in my body was flaring up all at once. The only family I had left was lecturing me about our parents' death, and it was killing me. I looked down at the gravel in the driveway, not daring to look anyone in the eye. "I…I gotta go."

I took off at a dead sprint toward the woods. I knew that I probably looked like a pathetic high school girl running from her problems, but I didn't care.

"Paige! Where are you going?" Niko yelled after me.

"To clear my head!" I shouted without looking back. I could feel the hot tears running down my face and a sharp pain in my heart. Everything that had happened lately was so overwhelming, and I needed to vent. I only made it so far into the woods before I fell to my knees and screamed into the darkness until my throat was on fire. My eyes were burning, my head was throbbing, and the screaming only relieved a little bit of pressure. I continued to cry as I leaned my back up against a tree and pulled my knees up to my chest in an attempt to comfort myself.

When something lightly touched my arm, I jumped. Through my tear-blurred vision, I could see William crouched down in front of me. His usual cocky smirk was gone, and it was the first time I ever saw a serious expression on his face. "I know that your brother touched a major nerve, but…I'm here if you need to talk or if you just need…someone. Can I sit down next to you?" he asked, not moving until I gave him an answer.

All I could manage was a weak nod, and he stood up to sit down at my side. I knew that Lily had probably sent him after me, but a part of me was just glad that he was there. I didn't have the words or the voice to say anything, so I just nuzzled into his side. He tensed up at my touch, but soon relaxed and put his arm around my shoulder awkwardly but also comfortingly. I started to cry again, and he gently stroked my hair. "Everything…everything is okay. It's all right to cry," he said in a soothing voice. His touch felt warm and safe, his voice was gentle and comforting, and him just being there was enough to make my pain slowly more bearable.

"W…William, can I…um can I talk to you about something?" When I spoke, my voice came out hoarse. My body was still trembling a little, but it was better than it had been.

"Yeah…Yeah, sure. Shoot." His voice was unsteady, kind of like he didn't know what to say. His words were awkward, and it gave me the impression that he had never really comforted anyone before.

"Well…when I was nine, my parents were assigned a big job. It required them to leave for a few days, but they had been away so much lately that when they told me, I just snapped. I threw things, I screamed at them, and I even told my mom that I hated her for leaving me alone. I ended up locking myself in my room and refusing to speak to them, so they took Niko to our grandfather's house and left for the job. I brooded around the house for a while, and a few days later, my current boss came by the house to give me an update on my parents' case. I got the worst news of my life. I was just a kid, and I was told that my mom and dad were never coming back. The last thing I had said to them was that I hated them, and I couldn't take that back. Me and Niko never spoke about our parents after that, and Niko got out of this life as soon as he could." I wasn't sure why

I was spilling my heart out to William. He was practically a stranger, someone I had only known for a few days, but there was some kind of connection. Maybe it was that I felt something for him, or maybe it was just that I needed someone to talk to, but it lifted a great weight off my shoulders.

He thought over everything I had said for a moment before responding in a quiet voice, "I don't want to cross any lines with you, but do you really think that beating yourself up over that fight for the rest of your life is what your parents would have wanted? I have lived for a very long time, and I know that if I got hurt or even passed on, that I would want everyone who cared about me to move on, live happy lives, no matter what they said or did to me in the past." My first impression of William was that he was cocky, arrogant, and an overall jerk, but I could see now that he did have a good heart like Grace said and just didn't know how to show his emotions very well. "Hey, would you mind…calling me Will? After so many hundred years, you get tired of the same name, and besides, most humans shorten their names nowadays anyway."

Even as he was speaking, I could feel myself drifting off. I was so tired, and I felt so warm and safe with him so close to me. "Sure, I can call you Will," I said right before the last of my tension melted away and I fell asleep.

I was gently jostled awake sometime later. I was no longer on the ground, and I was pressed firmly against someone's warm chest. I knew without even opening my eyes that it had to be William. He was carrying me, probably back to the house, and I nuzzled a little closer to him.

After a few moments of only listening to his slow, steady heart-beat, I started to hear hurried distant footsteps. Then I heard Niko's voice. "William you found her, thank the gods. Is she okay?"

I didn't bother opening my eyes; I didn't really want to have to talk to him. I was still mad, but I was too tired to try and sort out my problems at the moment.

I heard him stop right beside me and felt his cool hand cup the side of my face. "Yeah, she's okay. Just exhausted," William said, his voice right above my head.

26

"Thank you so much for going after her. Do you mind taking her to her room? You go up the stairs, and it's the first one on the right. Yours is right across the hall," Niko asked sincerely, but I could hear a hint of sorrow in his voice.

I heard the front door of the mansion open and the creak of floorboards before William answered, "Sure." That was all he said and headed up the stairs. He pushed open my door and gingerly laid me down on the bed. I know I should have expected it from Niko, but the mattress was one of the most comfortable things I'd ever laid on. "Saloth quaval, Paige," he whispered and gently patted me on the head. He turned to leave, but I mustered up the strength to grab the sleeve of his leather jacket.

"Will, what does that mean?" I asked as I looked up at him through my sleep-hazed vision.

He quietly laughed as he crouched down beside the bed. "It's Spanish for 'sleep soundly.'" He tucked a stray lock of my hair behind my ear before speaking again. "Now go back to sleep. I don't know what good it would do, but I'll go with you to talk to your brother tomorrow if you want."

"I know being nice isn't exactly your thing, so thank you, but I'll have to do that on my own. Sweet dreams Will," I said and pulled the blanket up to my shoulders.

He smiled at me once more before quietly leaving the room and shutting the door behind him.

CHAPTER 7

Apology before Breakfast

The next morning, I got up pretty early and took a much-needed shower. The closet in my room had clothes in it for me, and there was a lot to choose from. I ended up putting on a dark blue T-shirt with a denim jacket and a pair of faded blue jeans. I even dug through the bottom of the closet until I found an old pair of black biker boots to wear.

After getting dressed, I went downstairs and wandered around until I found the kitchen. Lily and Gabriel were sitting at the counter, making small talk.

"Good morning," I said, walking past them and heading straight for the coffeepot. I needed my morning caffeine something awful.

"Good morning, mon cheri. Are you okay? You gave us all quite the fright yesterday," Lily asked with a worried expression. It was nice of her to worry about me, but they didn't need to deal with my emotional baggage.

"Yeah, I'm fine, Lily, but I would like to talk to you guys about some stuff. First of all, where did you get those huge weapons yesterday? I knew you all had mystic weapons, but they practically showed up out of thin air." That was still very confusing, no matter how hard I thought about it.

"It is true that we all have our own weapons, and in their natural forms are quite hard to hide. That's why they have much smaller forms like this," Gabriel said, taking off his cufflinks and placing them on the counter in front of me.

At first, they just looked like normal gold cufflinks, but when I looked closer, I noticed that both of them very closely resembled tiny handguns. "How does something this small turn into something so deadly," I asked as I fumbled the links between my fingers.

"Well, first, you give them to the rightful owner," he said. Then he took them from me, stood up from his seat, and took a few steps away from us. "For us, we have to see and feel the weapon in our mind's eye, then I state my sin in Latin." He closes his eyes and holds out his hands, one cufflink in both of his open palms. "Cupiditas, appear and assist me." As soon as he finishes speaking, a dark green smoke rises in his hands, and in the blink of an eye, they turn into normal-sized handguns.

It was very cool, but I had to refrain from dropping my jaw in surprise or I was going to have black coffee down my front. "Do they all work like that?" I asked after taking another large gulp of my coffee.

Lily chuckled before responding, "Not quite, mon cheri. We are all different, so we use different languages. Mine just so happens to be French." She pulled the silver charm off her black velvet choker. "Luxure." The smoke that surrounded her hand was a mystifying violet, and in place of her charm was a shining silver rapier. She thrust it downward, and it whistled through the air. "Grace's chain and sickle turns into a bracelet, Simon's scythe turns into a sweatshirt charm, Preston's brass knuckles turn into rings, Elizabeth's metal whip turns into a bobby pin, and William's daggers turn into that dangly earring he wears all the time. If you'd like better training against sins, I'd be happy to oblige," she said and gave me a smirk that was anything but the motherly smile she usually had.

"Um...I think I'll pass, thanks," I said and reached for the coffeepot.

"Cupiditas, I'm done," Gabriel said, and the guns turned back into harmless cufflinks. As he clipped them back on his sleeves, he raised an eyebrow at the fact that I was refilling my mug. "You know, Paige, excessive amounts of caffeine are bad for your health, and I'm sure that it's safe to assume that that's not decaf."

A small tremor ran through my body. "Look, Gabriel, I know you're a doctor and all, but if you try to take my caffeine from me, I may have to hurt you." For the last five years, excessive amounts of black coffee was how I even managed to get to work in the mornings. The late nights, the early morning shifts, even the all-nighters—coffee was my best friend through it all, and right now I'm not sure I could go without it. Just going without it yesterday was rough.

Lily had already clipped her charm back onto her choker when Niko walked through the kitchen door. An awkward silence fell over the room, and no one dared to look anyone else in the eyes. Niko finally slightly lifted his head to speak to me. "Paige, will you come with me to the living room? We need to talk." His voice was firm, but his eyes were filled with guilt.

I didn't want to talk to him about what had happened, but I couldn't run from my problems forever. "All right," I said. Then I grabbed my coffee mug off the counter, slid off my stool, and followed him out of the kitchen. We walked down three different hallways until we reached a very spacious living room. There was a giant brick fireplace and luxurious leather furniture. The floor was spotless, and the walls were a calming dark red. I cautiously took a seat on the leather couch, and it was only about half as comfortable as it looked.

Niko paced back and forth in front of me for a moment, the tension visible in his posture. After a few seconds, he finally sat down next to me, but his gaze remained fixed on the floor. Now that he was sitting still, I could see that he was shaking. When he spoke, his voice was barely audible. "Listen Paige, I'm sorry about…about what I said about Mom and Dad. I'm just worried about you. I lost them and Grandpa too. I can't lose you. You're all I've got left, sis, and to think you're doing something so dangerous scares the hell out of me." He grabbed my free hand that was resting on the couch and squeezed it protectively, like at any moment I would disappear.

"I know, but someone has to do this job, and I'm not fifteen anymore. I promise I'm being very careful, and I'll visit more often if that would make you feel better, but I hate it when you're not smiling. A frown really doesn't suit your handsome face, which I would like to see if you're willing to look at me," I said and gently squeezed his hand in return. He hesitated, then looked at me, his features laced in guilt. "Hey," I said, wrapping my arms around his broad shoulders to gently hug him. "I'm not going anywhere, Niko. We have to look out for each other. Neither of us are ever going to be alone, okay?"

He wrapped me In a tight hug and nuzzled his face into my shoulder. After he took a few trembling breaths he nodded his head in agreement. I traced gentle circles on his back until his trembling stopped. He pulled away and looked me in the eyes with a small smile. "I'm glad you aren't angry at me. I, uh...I ordered this for you after talking with your friends. I didn't want to wait any longer to give it to you just in case you needed it." He reached into his jacket pocket and pulled out a phone with a dark green case, and the same sunflower charm that my old phone had was hanging off of it.

I took the phone in my hand and smiled. When our grandpa had given Niko and I our first phones, we got matching sunflower charms that clipped onto our cases. Every time we needed a new phone, we would always keep our charms. "You remembered. Where did you get this?"

"I have friends in high places. That's one of the times when being famous comes in handy. Your friends told me that your phone got...blown up, so I got you a new one, and it would be kind of weird if I was the only twin with a sunflower charm on their phone." Just then he pulled his phone out of his other jacket pocket, and a matching charm was hanging off it. His charm was a lot more worn than my new one, but I could still tell that they were a set. "I already put my number into your contact list, so you have no reason not to call me and invite me to celebrate with you when you ace this case."

"Thanks for believing in me...and for the new phone. We should probably go tend to our guests because this place is so big that if someone got lost in here, they would never be found," I said before hugging him once more and getting up from the couch. Then a thought hit me. "Oh crap. I should probably check in with Alex." I entered his number into my contact list and called him.

His phone didn't even ring. It just went straight to voice mail. "Hey, this is Alex Winters. I can't come to the phone right now, but if you leave a message, I'll get back to you as soon as I can. If this is an emergency, call my secretary at 538-488-9710."

I waited for the receiver to beep before I started speaking, "Hey, Alex, it's Paige. Just calling to check in. Everyone is fine, but call me back when you get this message so we can talk. Bye." I pocketed my phone, grabbed Niko's hand, and practically dragged him back to the kitchen.

CHAPTER 8

Bathing Suit

When we got back to the kitchen, Lily was busy at the stove, and the others were greedily chowing down on the best-smelling breakfast ever. Lily turned around with a spatula in her hand. "Oh, smiles suit you two perfectly. Are you in the mood for some aliments?"

I had almost forgotten every bit of my foreign language studies from grandpa, but I knew the word *food* in any language. "If it tastes even half as good as it smells, then yes please." I was starving and needed more coffee, but I could handle the coffee myself. As Lily added more pancake batter to her pan, I made my way over to the coffee maker. It was bone dry, so I started brewing a new batch.

I sat my mug down on the counter and called over to my brother, "Niko, do you want some coffee?" I chuckled at the thought of having to ask because he used to drink more coffee than me.

"No thanks, Paige. After my last doctor's visit, I have significantly decreased the amount of caffeine I drink," he said while pulling a carton of almond milk out of the fridge. Gabriel very obviously cleared his throat and continued eating. I could see him grinning around a mouthful of bacon even though he wasn't looking at me. I refilled my coffee mug, and on my way back across the kitchen, I swatted him on the head.

"Hey, what was that for?" he whined and rubbed his head where I smacked him.

I sat down at the end of the counter with the best indifferent look I could muster. "I warned you, Gabriel. If you try and take my caffeine away from me, I was going to hurt you," I said, crossing my legs.

The whole room erupted into laughter. Even Simon was having a hard time suppressing a chuckle, and Gabriel scowled while stuffing another piece of bacon in his mouth. It felt great to see everyone getting along and having a good time. If someone was looking at us from afar, we would have looked like a big family or a huge group of super close friends. I really miss hanging out with people I'm fond of, but I didn't have enough time to hang out with anyone due to my job, and it's hard to make close friends when you have to keep most of your life secret.

My indifferent expression shattered the moment Lily sat a stack of pancakes in front of me. They were the perfect golden brown with butter and loads of maple syrup. I stuck a bite in my mouth and practically melted out of my seat. "This is delicious! Lily, have I ever told you that you're amazing?" I asked, shoveling in bite after bite.

She chuckled while turning off the stove. "Thank you, mon cheri. Cooking for these six gives me a lot of practice."

Preston finished his breakfast and put his plate in the sink before voicing his question, "You wouldn't mind if we used the underground pool in your backyard, would you?"

I didn't even know that there was a pool in the backyard until he said something.

"I don't mind at all. Actually, if you all will follow me, we can get you some swimwear," Niko said and headed toward the doorway to the kitchen. We all put our dishes in the sink and followed my brother down the hall and into a gigantic walk-in closet. The rack on the right was filled with bikinis, and the rack on the left was filled with swim trunks. "I actually have an individual closet for each type of clothing that we use in my photo shoots. Most of the clothing, like this swimwear, is used once for a photoshoot, washed, and then never worn again. So feel free to use any of it that you like, and you can change in your bedrooms." Niko left us alone to choose what we wanted to wear.

There were tons of different sizes along with an assortment of colors and patterns. I had never worn a bikini before, but I had never gone swimming before either, so I flipped through the suits, looking for something that I liked. I finally found one that was brown with a turquoise rose pattern and a frilly skirt. I held it up to myself, and it looked like it'd fit just fine, so I went upstairs to my room and changed. It did fit pretty well, but I couldn't figure out how to tie the straps of the top. I heard someone moving in the hallway, and I was fed up with trying to tie the top myself, so I held up the top and poked my head out the door.

Grace and Lily were making small talk and heading toward the stairs. Grace's bikini was a flashy gold with black tiger stripes, and Lily's was rose colored and had ruffles all over it. "Um…Grace, Lily, can I have some help?" I'm sure my face was turning red with embarrassment, but it was better to ask them for help than having to ask the guys. Yikes, that would scar me for life.

Lily looked over at me and smiled. "Oh, sure, mon cheri. What's the matter?" Her and Grace walked over to my door, and I pulled it the rest of the way open.

"Well, you see…I, um, I'm having a little trouble with this bikini," I said and held up the strings behind my neck.

"Is that all? Turn around and I'll tie 'em for ya," Grace said, and I turned around. Without much effort at all, she tied the strings to where they were tight enough that it wouldn't come untied, but it wasn't so tight that it was pinching me.

When I turned back around to face them, Lily eyed my bathing suit, but her gaze lingered on my stomach. "That bikini looks good on you, and that birthmark is adorable," she said, and I glanced down at my side. I hardly noticed it anymore, but I had a birthmark on my right side that looked like an upside-down heart, and it wasn't much bigger than a bottle cap. I didn't know if it was because we were twins or what, but I knew that Niko had one too, and it was on his left side.

"Well, I don't know about you two, but I'm kind of interested to see what the guys look like in swim trunks. Gods, do you know how long it's been since Simon has worn anything besides sweatpants?" Grace said with a laugh. Then we all went to the backyard.

CHAPTER 9

Pool Problem

The pool was huge, with lounge chairs and umbrellas around it. Elizabeth's bikini looked like shiny lime-green snake scales, Preston's trunks were pitch black, Simon's were a faded blue green with black Zs on them, Gabriel's were striped yellow and orange, Will's were covered with flames, and Niko's were plain white. Everyone, including Spike and Duke, were in the pool except for Niko. He was in one of the lounge chairs tanning, a safe distance from the water.

I sat down on the edge of the pool and let my legs hang in the water. It was pretty hot outside, but the cool water washing over my skin felt amazing. Then I noticed that Will was swimming toward me. I could see every one of his abs flex with every step he took in my direction. All his muscles shimmered from the water droplets, and my mind went blank.

"Come on, Paige! It's no fun if you just sit on the edge. Get in the water!" he said, and before I had a chance to say anything, he grabbed my wrist and pulled me into the water. My head went under, and I started to panic. My mind went into survival mode, so he didn't have the chance to let go of my wrist before I grabbed hold of his arm and held on for dear life.

Then I heard a splash next to me, and a familiar set of muscular arms wrapped around my waist, pulling me to the surface. Once my head broke through the water, I greedily gasped for air to soothe my burning lungs. I wrapped my arms around Niko's neck and held on as tight as I could.

"It's okay. I got you," he said comfortingly. After I could breathe again, I glanced up at his face, but he wasn't looking at me. He was glaring at Will. Will looked rightfully confused. "I don't mind if you use my pool, but next time you want to drag someone in with you, ask them first." That last part came out very protective.

"I don't understand what I did wrong," he said, still confused. Will was obviously not the quickest on the uptake.

"Do I have to spell it out for you? Paige *can't swim*," my brother said, slightly tightening his grip on me. He had always been protective of me, but I had never seen him so angry before. Even if I include the time he found out that I was being bullied in elementary school.

I gently placed my hand on his shoulder. "It's okay, Niko. Will didn't know. He didn't mean me any harm. If anything, it's my fault for being a twenty-year-old who can't swim." I knew that it was pathetic that I didn't know how to swim, but I never had a reason to learn. "Just put me back on the edge and go back to your sunbathing." As expected, my brother did as I said, but not without a grumble of irritation.

Everyone went back to what they were doing, including Will. I guess he wasn't ready to be nice to me in front of other people yet, but that was okay. I got up, grabbed a towel, and wandered over to the bar next to the pool. As I slid onto one of the stools, one of Niko's housekeepers stood up and asked if I wanted anything.

"Give me the strongest virgin drink you can make," I said with a sigh. It was only one more day until my twenty-first birthday, but I still wasn't legally allowed to drink. I was going to have to get Niko something, or at least make him something.

As I waited for my drink, I carefully thought about what to do for my brother. What do you give someone who lives in a mansion and has enough money to buy whatever he wants? There weren't any stores around, so I would have to make something. The housekeeper set a cocktail glass in front of me. The drink looked like a rainbow of shaved ice with a tiny umbrella sticking out of it. The man handed me a spoon, and after a moment of hesitation, I took a bite. The ice felt nice and cool in contrast to the hot sun. The flavors were a mix of sweet and sour, but they all complemented each other perfectly.

After another half an hour of brainstorming and a few more of those rainbow drinks, I decide to go inside, change back to my normal clothes, and attempt to make Niko a cake. I grabbed an apron out of the cabinet and searched around the kitchen until I found all the ingredients that I needed. By the time I got everything mixed together, the kitchen was a complete disaster, so I just slid the cake pan into the oven and got as much flour off me as humanly possible. Then I sat down, and my mind started to drift. Me and the sins couldn't hide away in my brother's house forever, but I didn't know how to resolve the conflict without someone getting hurt or killed. Talking didn't work so well the last time, and I'd rather not go another round with Deseat's claws. I barely escaped getting sliced to ribbons the last time.

My thoughts were interrupted by the strong scent of something burning. "Oh crap!" I yelped and jumped out of my seat. I yanked the oven door open just to be punched in the face by a cloud of black smoke. My eyes and nose were watering, and I was coughing like crazy, but I managed to snatch a pot holder off the counter and pull the pan out of the oven. I tossed the pan of charcoal onto the counter and slammed the oven door shut.

Before I had much time to sulk about my complete failure of a cake, I heard Gabriel's voice in the hallway. "Oh my gods! What is that horrible smell?"

To my surprise, Lily was the one who strolled into the kitchen.

"Oh my, what happened in here?" she asked while glancing around at the mess I had made of the kitchen.

The jig was up. There was no excuse that I could come up with for why there was a pan of charcoal on my brother's counter. "I, uh…I burnt the, uh…birthday cake." I dropped the last words to a whisper. They didn't need to know about the whole birthday thing. It wasn't a big deal, but the beans were already way beyond spilled.

Lily grabbed a small towel off the counter, wetted half of it, and came over to hand it to me. "You have black ash all over your face. I assume the cake was for your brother?" she asked. I nodded while rubbing my face with the towel. "Well, if you want my help, all you have to do is ask, mon cheri."

I stopped cleaning my face and looked up at her with hopeful eyes. "I would be very grateful," I said and glanced back at the burnt pan. "I guess it's pretty obvious that I don't cook. I always had protein bars for breakfast, and I either skipped lunch or dinner and ate out for the meal I didn't skip."

"That is a horrible diet for someone your age, but let's not focus on that for now. You seem to have all the ingredients needed, so let's just make a new one," she said with a gentle smile.

With Lily's expert help, I had a simple yet beautiful cake sitting on the counter where the burnt pan had been within less than an hour. She had done most of the cooking, but I decorated it. It was a small vanilla cake with white icing and two rings of raspberries on top. She even helped me hide it behind some other things in the fridge. We cleaned up the kitchen together, which took a while with the disaster I had made of it, and wandered off to the living room.

Gabriel, Niko, and William were playing rummy at the coffee table in front of the couch. Gabriel had a stack of twenty dollar bills sitting on the table next to him. It was obvious that he had won every game prior to when we had arrived. Niko was shuffling the deck when Lily and I sat down on the floor across the table from them. "Want to join in the next game?" Gabriel asked with a mischievous smirk.

Both of us agreed, and as soon as the next game started, it ended with me as the victor. "How the hell did you win already? Not to boast, but I do a lot of gambling for a reason, and Lily and Gabriel are even better than me at cards," William said in an utterly baffled tone. "That has to be beginner's luck," he said while crossing his arms with a huff of irritation. He was kind of cute when he pouted.

Niko chuckled at his reaction, and I just grinned. "Let's just say we played a lot of cards when we were younger. You want to play another round?" I snatched up the deck of cards and started shuffling them. As I expected, none of them were willing to back down yet, except for Niko because he already knew there was no chance of him winning. After about a dozen more games, a.k.a. about a dozen more losses, they finally gave up, and we all decided that it was time to hit the hay.

When I got back up to my room, I kicked off my boots and flopped onto the bed with a sigh. I checked my phone, but Alex still hadn't called me back yet, so I plugged in my phone and got up to get ready for bed. There was a bathroom attached to my bedroom, and it just made getting ready for bed so much easier. When I finally lay back down and turned off the light, I was so tired and relaxed that I wasn't alone with my thoughts long before I drifted off to sleep.

CHAPTER 10

Cafe Brise De Mer

The next morning, I woke up to someone knocking on my door. I moaned as the light shining in the window blinded me.

"Who is it?" I groaned in dismay.

"It's me. Can I come in?" The sound of Will's voice made my eyes fly wide open.

"H...hang on just a second," I stammered out. I had felt so comfortable the night before that I had slept in nothing but my underwear and bra! I tried to get out of bed, but I was still half asleep, and my legs were tangled up in the blanket. I stumbled a few steps from the bed and fell to the ground with a loud thud. "Owww."

"Paige, is everything all right in there?" Will called from the hallway.

My butt was killing me, but I wasn't going to tell him that. "Just peachy. I'll be out in a minute," I said, struggling to detangle myself from the blanket. Once free, I jumped to my feet and ran to the closet. I threw on a pair of jeans and a gray T-shirt, then I went back to the bed to pull on my boots. I quickly ran a brush through my hair and grabbed my phone off the charger before yanking the door open.

I was still breathing heavily from trying to get ready so fast, and Will just stared at me in surprise. "Well, good morning to you too. I wanted to apologize for yesterday and ask if you were ready for breakfast." As soon as he finished his sentence, my stomach growled. I turned away from him because I knew my face was turning red with embarrassment. *Nice going, stomach. I know you're hungry, but you didn't have to agree so loudly.*

"Don't worry about it, and breakfast sounds great," I said around a nervous chuckle. At least he had the courtesy to apologize to me even if it wasn't in front of the others.

He laughed at me playfully under his breath. "Actually I planned to take you back to the city to celebrate your birthday…if that's okay with you."

Of course Lily couldn't keep her mouth shut. Why did I expect her to? "Well, I guess that's okay as long as we keep from drawing too much attention to ourselves and we make it back before dark."

"Yeah, yeah, I know the rules, Mom. Drive the speed limit, obey street signs, and don't drink alcohol when you have to drive home. I got it," he said in a mocking tone that made me burst into laughter. "And you don't have to worry about the whole drawing attention thing. It's just going to be me and you."

Wait, just me and him? Is he…is he asking me out on a date? No way, he's probably just trying to be nice again and not realizing that it sounds like a date because he is so dense when it comes to emotions. A girl can still dream though, right? He started walking toward the stairs and motioned for me to follow. "Shouldn't we tell the others that we're leaving?" I trotted down the stairs close behind him.

"No need. I already talked to Gabriel and your brother, which I'm pretty sure he still doesn't like me," he said as he held the front door open for me. That was unusual because Niko didn't hold grudges, but he was also very protective of me.

"Don't worry, I'm sure he'll come around eventually." Will had just shut the front door when my phone started beeping. When I pulled it out of my pocket and checked the screen, I saw that Alex was trying to call me. "It's my boss. You go on over and get the bike ready. I'll be over in a minute." Will just shrugged and walked away. Then I swiped my finger over the phone screen and held it to my ear. "Hey, Alex, what's up?"

"Hi, Paige. I'm sorry that I didn't respond to your call. I was in a meeting and forgot to turn my ringer back on afterwards. Is everything still okay wherever you are?" he asked.

"Everything's fine here, but have the lesser sins caused any more trouble lately?" I really needed to get back to the task that I was given, but it was so easy to just forget about it. As crazy as it may sound, I felt more normal with the major seven than I ever had. Maybe it was because they treated me like family.

"Surprisingly no. They're being unusually quiet. I assume that they're still looking for you guys, which means your hiding place must be pretty friggin' amazing," he said with a chuckle. Then I heard shouting on the other end of the line. "Crap! Someone get some sedatives. Why are they in here? Sorry, Paige, having a little bit of vampire trouble at the moment. Gotta go. Stay alive and check in!"

That was the last thing I heard before he hung up. It was entertaining to think that a little over a week ago, I was dealing with minor cases like that, and now I'm up the creek without a paddle.

My attention was drawn away from my phone when I heard the motorcycle engine revving. "You ready to go?" Will called over to me with a smirk.

I looked down at my phone screen once more before sliding it into my pocket and running over to Will. "I'm ready." After slipping his helmet on, I got on his motorcycle, and we drove off.

It didn't take long before the city came into view, but as soon as it did, Will slowed down to the speed limit. It was strange because he seemed like such a speed demon up until then. "Why did you slow down?" I asked, finding it easier to speak to him at this speed.

"You said to keep a low profile, right? What better way to start then obeying the speed limit?" he asked with a chuckle that I could actually hear. I really liked it when he drove like a daredevil, but just cruising like this was kind of nice too.

The first place we went when we got into the city was...Gabriel's clinic? I was completely baffled when Will drove us into the alley next to the clinic and turned off the motorcycle. He got off and took the helmet off my head to clip it on the saddlebag. "Why exactly are we at Gabriel's clinic?" I finally asked when he motioned for me to follow him out of the alley.

I didn't even notice the giant piece of fence leaning against the side of the building until Will pulled it across the opening of the alley. There were older chains bolted to both walls right next to the opening. With both of us on the outside, Will chained the fence in place. Then he turned to look at my puzzled expression. "This way we don't have to worry about the lesser sins finding my motorcycle, and I don't have to worry about some punk kid trying to steal it. What do you want for breakfast?"

I thought about it for a long moment, then I remembered that there was a little café a few blocks away. "Hey, why don't we go to Cafe Brise de Mer?"

He stopped walking and gave me a puzzled look. "I have no idea where that is or what that means. All I know is it's not Spanish."

I chuckle at his confusion before taking his hand and pulling him in the direction of the cafe. "It's French for 'Cafe Sea Breeze.' The first time I went there, I had to ask one of the cashiers what it meant too," I said with a smile. He didn't say anything else but gently squeezed my hand in return.

CHAPTER 11

Cream Cheese

When we pushed open the doors of the café, the strong scent of cinnamon and coffee beans filled my nose. To anyone else, those smells would be insignificant, but they were very calming to me. The counter was completely made of glass, and the layers of display cases below it were filled with every type of pastry imaginable. I looked over at Will, and he was gazing at everything in amazement. Then he turned toward me. "How do you pick just one of these? I swear, this is making me want to go into a food coma."

"It is pretty hard to choose, but I just try to think about what I want to taste the most. I think…" I paused and glanced at the coffee options. "I think I'll get a blueberry cream cheese Danish and a coffee with cream. Will, what are you going to get?"

"Um…I guess I'll get the same. Just don't add cream to my coffee," he said with an unsure look on his face.

I smiled at him, and as I reached into my back pocket for the cash my brother had given me, Will handed a credit card over the counter. "Will, I could have paid for it. I was the one who suggested we come here."

He laughed as he slid the card back in his jacket pocket. "Don't worry about it. It's your birthday, and besides, it's Gabriel's card anyway. I may have snuck it out of his jacket while we were talking this morning."

I was surprised. I knew he was the bad boy type, but I wasn't expecting him to actually steal his brother's credit card. Before I had time to say anything, the cashier handed us our breakfast, and my mind lost all other thoughts except for how hungry I was. We sat down at a small table near the window. The sunlight streaming in was warm and gentle.

The Danish was really good, and the bitterness of the coffee was a great contrast to the sweet cream cheese. When I looked up at Will, he had already scarfed down his Danish and half of his cup of coffee, but looked satisfied with both. Then I noticed that he had a little bit of cream cheese right on the end of his nose. I couldn't suppress a chuckle over the fact that it made him look like a little kid.

He gave me a wide-eyed, oblivious stare, and I couldn't suppress my laughter any longer. "What? What's so funny?"

It took me a second to gain enough composure to actually form words around my laughter. Seeing him like that was just way too cute. "You...you have cream cheese on your nose." He quickly retched up to wipe it off and turned away from me, but I could swear that I saw the faintest hint of a blush coloring his face.

After we both finished up our breakfast, we decided to stay in the cafe until we could figure out what we were going to do next. It only took a few moments for me to be buried deep in my own thoughts. There weren't really a lot of options. We couldn't go to confined spaces with lots of people, which ruled out shopping, museums, and movie theaters. Not to mention that Will would probably want to do something at least a little bit exciting, so no walks in the park and no orchestra performances. My mind came down to three options, and if we timed it right, we could probably do all of them.

"All right Will, how about we space out ice skating, bowling, and the amusement park throughout the day?"

"I don't think ice skating would be a good idea because it would be hard to get away if we ran into trouble, and bowling wouldn't be very fun with only two of us, but the amusement park might be fun," he said with a grin. Something about him made me feel like he was in a better mood than usual, and I didn't think it was because of the Danish.

Ten blocks later, we found ourselves at the only amusement park in the city. Sunyshore Amusement Park had been in the city longer than I could remember. I used to go there with my parents, and even our grandfather took me and Niko there a few times before he died. The giant metal entryway had started to collect rust, and we could tell that the booths hadn't been remodeled in a while, but that was okay with me. The place wasn't crowded, but it wasn't deserted either. There were quite a few families rushing from ride to ride and even some elderly couples here and there eating sweet treats or just enjoying a walk through the park.

CHAPTER 12

Darts and the Devil's Tail

"Well, Paige, what do you want to do first?" Will asked.

I glanced around at our surroundings, at first not sure whether I wanted to ride something or play a game. Then I remembered one specific ride from when I was younger. It was called the Devil's Tail, and it was the fastest and most thrilling ride in the entire park. It only seemed fitting to take Will on that ride first. "Let's go ride the Devil's Tail."

His face practically lit up with excitement. "Yes! I half expected you to be one of those girls who wouldn't ride roller coasters because they were 'too much.'" Him making quotation marks with his fingers just made it feel like more of an insult.

"Have you met me? If I was that kind of girl, I would have given up on this case the minute I met you," I said and playfully punched him in the arm.

"Fair point." His smile with those words made my heart race, and he took my hand to lead me through the park. I was a little surprised that the ride wasn't closed down, but less surprised that the waiting line was super short. When I was a kid, people would be too afraid to ride this roller coaster, and now there were only a few teenagers in line ahead of us.

Will and I were seated right next to each other, and right after we got situated, the safety bars locked in place tightly across our chests. Then we started slowly climbing up the first hill, and my anticipation continued to grow the closer we got to the top. Will must have been able to tell because he grabbed my hand and laced his fingers with mine. As soon as we reached the top and started to descend, I felt my stomach drop, and I couldn't hold back a thrilled scream, but I was shocked when I heard Will excitedly screaming right alongside me. The wind was whipping my hair back and forth, and all the scenery around us was zipping by in a blur. At every sharp turn, corkscrew, and hill, I felt like the only thing holding me in the seat was Will's hand linked with mine, but the adrenaline rush felt amazing.

Due to its speed, the ride was over before we knew it. As we stepped off the ride, I glanced over at Will, who had a pleased smile glued to his face. "You look like you enjoyed that." At my words, he turned away with a faint blush. I laughed and decided to change the subject. "Note to self, tie your hair back before getting on a roller coaster."

"I could have told you that, and I can't do anything with my hair because it sticks straight out in every direction. Well, what do you want to do next? We can play some games. Maybe I can win you a teddy bear or something," he said, much more comfortable with the topic of conversation.

I quirked one eyebrow at him. "Do I look like the kind of girl who needs a guy to win her a teddy bear? How about I win you a teddy bear?"

He gave me a competitive smirk. "Is that a challenge? I guarantee you I'll win, mi cielo."

"What does that mean?" I asked, half expecting him to be cursing at me in Spanish.

"It means 'my heaven.'"

I was surprised but also touched that he had given me a cute nickname.

Then we both made a beeline for the nearest competition booth, and it just so happened to be a dart-throwing booth. I handed the vender four dollars, which in turn got each of us two darts. The objective was to throw the darts one at a time and get as close to the center as possible. If you hit the center circle, then you win a stuffed animal of your choice, but if you're playing against someone, it's based on a normal point system. When I looked at Will, he was giving me an all-too-knowing smile.

"You already paid, so you can't back out now, but need I remind you what my mystical weapons are?" he said with a chuckle. Oh crap. I completely forgot that his mystical weapons were throwing knives. That's it; I'm done for. He's going to hit the center every time, but I'm not going down without a fight!

I covered my moment of panic with a grin. "I know what they are, but that doesn't scare me. If you haven't figured it out, I'm very stubborn, and I *will* beat you."

That brought a genuine laugh out of him, deep and crisp. His eyes were lit up with the excitement of a challenge, but there was something else in them too. Something warm, something gentle, something almost…joyous? His smile made a blush creep up the back of my neck, and I could feel my face growing warm. Will's smile grew even deeper. "You know, you're cute when you blush, mi cielo."

I knew my entire face had to be cherry red, and there wasn't any way to cover it up, so I just turned back toward the targets in front of us. I threw my first dart, and it hit the outer ring. About a centimeter to the left and I would have missed the target completely. Will had distracted me, and he knew it too. I glared at him, but he just smirked in mock innocence.

"You must really want to lose if that's the best you've got." He threw his first dart without breaking eye contact with me. He just barely missed the center and laughed to himself. "I'm getting a little rusty. All of this having to behave myself crap is putting me out of shape. Well, go ahead and throw your other dart so I can win."

I looked back at the target with determination. I had taken target training back at SAHRA, but that was with the handgun I carried in my purse before it got blown up. *Okay, I need to think calming thoughts, think calming thoughts.* The first thing that came to mind was camping out under the stars with the cool wind brushing my face, the sweet scent of wildflowers tickling my nose, and crickets chirping their midnight tunes. I closed my eyes to picture it in my mind, and when I opened them, the image was still there. The only difference was the target in front of me, and it was lit up like a beacon. I centered up the target, said a silent prayer to the gods, and threw the dart.

By some God-given miracle, I hit the target dead center and couldn't hold back a whoop of victory. I turned toward Will and stuck out my tongue like a little kid. "Take that! I believe that I have won, so you can go cry in a corner now."

"Not so fast, hotshot. I still have one dart left," he said, twiddling the dart between his fingers like he was performing a knife trick. Really? He had another dart, and I just made a complete fool of myself? That's just great! He looked at the target and threw his dart. As expected, his dart hit the center, knocking mine loose and sending it to the ground. He won fair and square, but that didn't make me any less irritated that he had beat me after I was so determined to win.

"What stuffed animal would you like sir?" The vendor's voice is what pulled me out of my thoughts and back to reality.

"Um, how about that one," Will said, pointing at a small black teddy bear with red devil horns and wings. Of course he would pick the one that looked like a demon. The man grabbed the bear and handed it to Will, who held it out to me. I was surprised that he was giving it to me, but at the same time, I was happy that he was giving me a gift.

CHAPTER 13

Don't Judge

I took the bear and held it close to my chest. "Thank you," I mumbled, my pride losing to my feelings for him. Then I noticed that the bear was a key chain and clipped it to one of my belt loops. I don't know why I felt so fond of him. After this case, I probably wouldn't ever see him again. That thought was more painful than I ever thought it could be, and I had to fight back the urge to cry.

My depressed thoughts must have been showing on my expression because Will spoke up in a concerned tone, "Paige, is something wrong?"

I immediately smiled at him and glanced around for something to change the subject. "No, I'm fine. Why don't we go get some, uh…" Then I caught sight of a small cotton candy stall a little ways away. "Let's go get some cotton candy." I headed toward the stall a little faster than I meant to, but Will was in a good mood for once, and I wasn't about to ruin it.

As soon as the sugary scent hit my nose, I realized just how much I actually wanted it. I hadn't had cotton candy since I was young, and I'd given up most sugary treats when I started working at SAHRA because I had to stay in shape. Why do the best-tasting things have to be the worst for you?

I handed the woman a five-dollar bill, and in return, she handed me two bundles of cotton candy. When I got back to Will, I held both of them up and asked, "Do you want the pink or blue?"

"I'm more partial to the blue myself. I always thought that it tasted better than the pink," he said, plucking the blue cotton candy out of my hand and taking a bite out of it. I did the same to the pink one, and the sweet strawberry fluff dissolved on my tongue. "Hey, we should probably get something for lunch too. I'm starting to get hungry."

"Hmm…I'm kind of in the mood for a cheeseburger and French fries. Oh, and a vanilla milkshake, if we can find a booth that sells milkshakes," I said, and my stomach growled. I didn't even realize that it was time for lunch until he said something about it, but I was actually hungry too.

We wandered around until we both got what we wanted to eat for lunch and we found a table to sit at. Will ended up getting chicken legs, deep fried pickles, and a can of beer. We laid our food out on the table and dug in. My cheeseburger was really good, but Will gave me a baffled look when I started dipping my fries in my milkshake. "What?"

"Why are you dunking your fries in your milkshake? That doesn't even sound like it would taste good," he said and shoved another pickle in his mouth.

"Whoa, whoa, whoa. Don't knock it till you've tried it. French fries dipped in milkshakes are amazing! My grandfather first showed me that trick when I was eleven and we stopped at a fast-food restaurant after an archery lesson. I've loved fries with milkshakes ever since." Will shook his head and took a drink of his beer. "I don't get why you drink that stuff. It smells so bitter."

Then a mischievous smirk spread across his face. "I tell you what, mi cielo. If you take a drink of my beer, then I will eat some of your…milkshake fries."

"Okay. I mean, one drink won't kill me, and you'll see how amazing these are." I handed him a few fries and my milkshake while he handed me his beer. It smelled even more bitter up close, but he was trying my fries, so I had to try it. I took a swig and swished it around in my mouth for a minute. It really didn't taste that bad. In fact, it kind of tasted like coffee with a flavorful zing to it, which I thought was kind of nice. I took another sip out of the can, and another, and another. Then I noticed that Will was sneaking more fries out of my box and dipping them in my milkshake. "Hey, I'd like to have some of that left when you're done."

Will looked up at me with a fry hanging out of his mouth. I could see a blush creeping up his face, and he started to stammer out a response, "I, uh, I could say the same to you. You seem to be enjoying that beer, and as much as I don't want to admit it, these are actually pretty good."

"I told you so, and your beer isn't half bad either." I smiled at him, and we shared the rest of our meals with each other. After we finished eating, we went to a few more booths waiting for our food to settle before going from ride to ride for a couple hours.

CHAPTER 14

Uninvited Guests

When we stepped off our last ride, I felt something cold and wet drip onto my face. I looked up, and I saw that storm clouds had gathered overhead without us even noticing. It really started to pour, then Will grabbed my hand and pulled us under the awning of a nearby closed-down booth. After a few minutes, it started getting cold, and I began to shiver. The temperature hadn't been too bad earlier, but the rain had completely soaked through my clothes. In response, Will took off his jacket, slid it over my shoulders, and pulled me so close to his side so that I was leaning against him. He was so warm, and his jacket gave off the comforting scent of his cologne.

All of a sudden, I felt Will's index finger slide under my chin and tilt my face up toward his. The usual mischief in his eyes was gone, and they were now burning bright with passion. Was he really about to do what I thought he was about to do? He stopped only a few inches from my face and brushed his thumb across my bottom lip as if asking for permission. My entire face was on fire, but I managed a slight nod. He quickly closed the distance between us, and our lips met in a desperate kiss. The cool metal of his lip ring was a stark difference to the heat of his lips. It started out gentle, but then grew deeper to the point of me being able to feel his passion between our lips. When our lips finally parted, he pressed his forehead against mine and smiled.

"I've wanted to do that for so long, mi cielo. I've been with countless other girls, but I've never felt like this with anyone else.

I feel…I feel like you fill a hole in my heart that I never realized I had. You bring out the best in me, and as selfish as it sounds, I don't want that feeling to go away. I don't want you to leave me," Will said, his voice trembling. His bad boy mask had shattered, and his eyes were burning with pure raw emotion. Then I saw a tear slide down his cheek.

I was completely awestruck until I realized that he was waiting for me to respond. I couldn't keep a smile from spreading across my face. "I feel the same way." Then I chuckled. "Well, maybe not about being with countless other girls, but…I don't want you to leave me either."

That brought a chuckle out of him too, and he gently kissed me again before pulling me into a tight embrace. I was overwhelmed with joy. I was so glad that he felt the same way and it wasn't just an act. My fingers curled tightly into his wet T-shirt as I returned his embrace.

Then I felt every muscle in his body go rigid, and he pulled away from me but slid his hand into mine. "We have unwanted company," he said while glancing around suspiciously. When I looked out across the park, there was a group of angry people headed in our direction through the rain. They had to be sins because pretty much everyone else had left to get out of the rain, and they weren't wearing security uniforms.

"Come on, I was having a good day for once! It's like they know when the worst time to interrupt us is. What are we going to do now?" I asked, irritation flowing through every fiber of my being.

"We're going to have to find a roundabout way back to my motorcycle, but for right now, let's just get out of here." He took off running toward the entrance of the amusement park, pulling me closely behind him. We were almost there when we noticed more sins standing at the gateway. Will stopped dead in his tracks and started glancing around for some place to hide.

Then I spotted the entrance to the house of horrors not too far from where we were standing. "There," I said, pointing toward the building. We sprinted as fast as we could to the door and ducked through. Once inside, I realized I might have preferred to take my chances out in the rain with the sins. I knew the house was meant to scare people, but it was seriously giving me the creeps, and the storm raging outside wasn't helping. There weren't any lights on, and most of the jump scares probably weren't working because the house of horrors was supposed to be closed down.

We ran up the stairs and were looking for a place to hide when we heard the front door burst open downstairs. Then we heard shouting and stomping around. I dropped my voice to an anxious whisper. "Crap! Will, if we just stand here, they're going to find us in no time."

At the sound of my voice, he pulled me over to the far wall and pushed over a candlestick that had been sitting on a small coffee table covered in fake cobwebs. The wall creaked and slid open to reveal a small closet-like space that I would have never guessed was there. It was a tight squeeze for us both to fit, but once we were both inside, Will slid the panel back into place. We were so close that I could feel his breath ruffling my hair. There was a sharp pain in my thigh where his knee was pressed up against it, but there wasn't any room for either of us to move over. I tried to shift my weight, but every time I moved, the floor would creak and the pain in my thigh would just get worse. My leg started to go numb. "Will, I can't feel my—"

He gently covered my mouth with his hand. "Ssshhh, mi cielo. They'll hear you."

I hadn't even noticed that the footsteps had moved up to the second floor and were moving around in the same room as us. It felt like alarm bells were going off in my chest, and I was sure that Will could hear them, or at least feel them. I buried my face in his chest to try and muffle my breathing that I knew was too loud as the footsteps walked right over to the wall we were hiding behind. I felt Will's arms tighten around me, and it made me feel a little safer.

"Where are they! They couldn't have just disappeared! Search the whole park if you have to, but find them!" The voice had a venomous bite to it that sounded just like Deseat, and it was right on the other side of the wall. It felt like hours before the footsteps left the room and the house grew quiet.

Will slightly cracked the panel open and looked around before completely pushing it aside. "Come on, we have to get out of here before they come back," he said as we detangled ourselves and stepped out of the wall. My leg was still completely asleep, and it crumpled under me when I put weight on it. With surprising quickness, Will wrapped his arm around my waist and kept me from falling. "Whoa, are you all right?" His face was drawn tight with concern.

"I'm fine, my leg is just asleep. How did you know that opening was there?" The numbness in my leg had started to fade to a tingling sensation that told me it was waking up.

"Believe it or not, I worked here for a solid month a few years ago, and I memorized every nook and cranny of this entire house. I loved scaring the absolute dog crap out of those little kids, but the boss said he kept getting complaints about me taking it too far, so he fired me. I'm just glad it was still there," he said and helped me over to the stairs.

Not that I didn't love the close proximity, but we weren't going to be able to sneak out of here very easily if he had to support my weight the whole time, so I pulled away from him ever so slightly. "I can walk now. What's the plan?"

"Well, I say we sneak out the back door and behind the booths until we get to the fence, then I cut it open and we'll make a beeline for my motorcycle." He started down the stairs, and I quietly followed after him. With every step, the floorboards would creak under us, but it was barely audible over the raging storm outside.

His plan sounded all fine and dandy, but I had a question lingering in my mind. "Hey, um, maybe I'm wrong, but shouldn't we confront them? I mean, trying to talk to them didn't work out so well for me last time, and I'm not exactly eager to try it again, but... can't you fight them off or get it into their thick skulls that you aren't giving up your position as the sin of Wrath to anyone?"

He stopped right next to the back door and chuckled at me. "Look, I've been the sin of Wrath since...always. Even if they managed to kill me, there's no telling what would happen because no one ever has before, and even though I love starting fights, I'm not suicidal. There are entirely too many of them and only one of me, so we are going to sneak out of here, end of story."

Before I had the chance to comment, he pushed the door open, and my jaw snapped shut. I didn't want to take the chance of anyone hearing us, so I didn't say another word. We crouched down and snuck out the door, making sure to not let it slam behind us. We had to creep along a narrow sidewalk because that was the only thing in between the back of the house of horrors and the canal that ran through the center of the park. I could hear the distant shouting of the sins searching for us, but I couldn't see anyone through the thick rain. I took one uneven step, and my foot slid out from under me, which caused me to tumble into the railing. I silently thanked the gods that it was there because otherwise I would've fell right into the canal.

Will turned back toward me and mouthed, "Are you okay?" He extended his hand to help me off the railing.

I nodded at him and mouthed back, "Yeah."

I took his hand and righted myself. When he turned back to lead the way, I grabbed ahold of the hem of his wet T-shirt. He glanced at me over his shoulder but didn't protest and continued leading us to the exit.

CHAPTER 15

Masked Surprise

After a while of sneaking around behind booths and through rides in the rain, we finally came up to the fence. He took out his earring and held it loosely in the palm of his hand. Will whispered, "Ira," and a small golden dagger appeared in place of the earring. It had beautiful designs carved into it, and there were tiny rubies set into the handle in the shape of a lovely intricate dragon. He cut a piece out of the fence with ease, and we slipped through. "La Ira se desvanece."

I assumed that was his way of dismissing his weapon because the dagger vanished in a poof of bloodred smoke. With the dagger once again in its harmless tiny form, he clipped it back on his ear. He took my hand and laced our fingers together with a smirk. We ran around the city for a while, down alleys, and across side streets just in case someone had followed us.

By the time we got back to his motorcycle, the rain had stopped, and the sun was making its last streaks of red in the sky. "I hope the others don't get mad that we're a little late getting back," he said while pushing the fence out the way and tossing me the helmet.

Why would the others be mad? I didn't tell them that I was going to be back before dark; I only told Will. I didn't have enough time to question it because he revved the engine and motioned for me to get on.

The drive back was as short and peaceful as it always was, and the moon had started to rise by the time we pulled into my brother's driveway. When Will turned off the motorcycle, I climbed off and tossed the helmet onto one of the handle grips. He started walking toward the house, but I grabbed his hand so he would turn around and look at me.

"I had a really good time today. Probably the best birthday ever, even with all the sins drama. I actually kind of enjoyed hiding and sneaking around with you, but I still hate them for interrupting us." I felt my face heat up as my mind went straight to the memory of Will kissing me in the rain.

A devilish smirk drew across his face, and he reached up to cup my cheek in his hand. "Well, we could pick up where we left off."

I smiled back at him, and he pulled me into a deep kiss. This time, I hardly even noticed that his lip ring was there. I was too wrapped up in the moment. I couldn't resist the urge to reach up and run my fingers through his hair. Despite it looking like it would stab you if you touched it, his hair was surprisingly soft. He kept his one hand gently holding my face while the other one slid down my spine to rest in the small of my back. When I caught a glimpse of his eyes, they were glowing red with desire. A shiver ran down my spine when his tongue forced its way between my teeth and started playing with mine.

Then the mansion's door flew open, and we jumped away from each other, still panting from the rush. My skin was still tingling where his hands had been.

"William!" Lily was marching toward us, and she did not sound happy. "You had one job, one job! Be back before dark, and you show up a half an hour after the sun had already gone down. Paige is now late to her own party!"

Will looked like he was only about half listening, but I heard her loud and clear. "Party? What party?" I hadn't noticed it before because Lily always dressed in fancy clothing and I was too flustered about her almost seeing our make-out session, but she was wearing a faded purple ball gown, matching gloves that went up to her elbows, white heels, and large decorative feathers were pinned in her hair.

Lily turned around and smiled at me. "You'll find out soon enough, mon cheri. We have to get you ready first." She grabbed my wrist and started pulling me in the direction of the mansion.

I was completely at a loss for words, and when I looked at Will, he just smiled and waved at me. "Have fun being tortured by my older sister."

"Oh no you don't, mister," Lily said, grabbing him by the arm and dragging him along with us. "You have to get ready too. The guys are waiting for you in the kitchen, and I'm eager to see what you look like when they're done." As much as Will tried to protest, Lily completely ignored him.

Lily left Will and his jacket, which I had still been wearing, at the bottom of the stairs and led me to a room on the second floor. Grace and Elizabeth were waiting for us in the room, dressed in outfits that were just as extravagant as Lily's. Elizabeth's gown was super frilly and a gentle summer-green color. Also her short blonde hair was put up in an elegant bun. Grace was wearing a tight-fitting sequined gown that sparkled like gold. Plus, her black hair was down and had recently been permed.

The dresser was covered in cosmetics, hair products, and an array of fancy perfumes. "Come over here and sit down, mon cheri. I've been dying to do your makeup and hair ever since we met," Lily said, indicating a chair sitting in front of the dresser's large mirror. "Where did you get this little bear?" she asked while gently taking it off my belt loop and setting it on the dresser.

"Oh, Will won it at one of the amusement park booths today and gave it to me," I told her, and to my surprise, she gave me a knowing smile. All three of them set to work on getting me ready for whatever party they had planned. It felt really strange because I hardly ever did my own makeup, let alone had someone else do it.

After them fussing back and forth about my appearance for the better part of a half an hour, they helped me into a gown and let me look in the mirror. I hardly recognized the person staring back at me. The dress was midnight blue. The top was made out of lace with an off-my-shoulders long-sleeved style, and the back was open about halfway down my spine. The skirt of the dress went all the way down to my ankles, and it shimmered when the light hit it just right. It was probably the fanciest and most beautiful thing I had ever worn. My hair was loosely braided, and Elizabeth had given me a pair of basic black heels. Lily had given me a silver chain necklace with a moon-shaped diamond charm and matching earrings that went with the gown perfectly. They hadn't put a ton of makeup on me, but they did a flawless job with my mediocre face.

Just then there was a knock at the door. "Are you ladies finished yet? I would like to have a moment alone with my sister." It was Niko's voice, but he didn't even attempt to open the door without one of the girls answering him.

Lily looked at me for permission, and when I nodded, she opened the door and stepped out of the way for him to see me. "Say hello to the new and improved Paige Striffe."

Niko was dressed in an old-time suit with a black tailcoat and a black masquerade mask. Also his hair was down and parted on the side. When he saw me, his jaw literally dropped open in amazement. Grace giggled at his expression, then Lily said, "Elli, Grace, we should head down to the party."

They left the room after showering me with hugs, waves, and giggles and quietly closed the door behind them.

It took a second for Niko's shock to wear off before he spoke, "You look...amazing." I felt my face flush as I looked toward the ground. Then I saw something in his hand. He must have noticed that I was staring at it because he glanced down and then held it out to me. "Uh, happy birthday," he stammered out. I took the small rectangular box out of his hand and opened it to reveal an interesting-looking hairpin. The part that was supposed to go into my hair was shaped like a knife, but the top looked like a beautifully intricate black rose with tiny silver chains hanging from it and a small clear crystal set in the center.

"Niko, it's so beautiful. I love it, but why does it look like a knife?" I asked, slightly confused.

"Hey, I said that I was okay with you continuing your job, not that I was going to turn off my protective brother complex. May I?" he asked, indicating that he would put it in my hair for me. I nodded and turned around. He slid the pin into the top of my braid, and I couldn't even feel the knife blade because he intertwined it with my hair. When I turned back around, he was holding up a black-and-silver masquerade mask. "You're going to need this before we head down to the party."

I put the mask on, and Niko led me down stairs to a ballroom that I didn't even know was part of the mansion.

CHAPTER 16

Downhill Masquerade

The second we stepped through the double doors, we were attacked by the cheers of the major seven and everyone who worked in my brother's mansion. There were tons of tables covered in champagne glasses, party food, and even the cake Lily and I made for Niko was there. Lily, Grace, and Elizabeth were now wearing masks that matched their dresses. Gabriel was wearing a dark green suit and tie with a matching mask that only covered one side of his face, and he was carrying around a full champagne glass. Simon must not have been on board with the whole suits thing because he wasn't wearing one, but he did put on a nice pair of jeans, dress shoes, a turquoise button-up shirt, and a simple mask that was the same color as his shirt. Preston had on a normal black suit minus the tie, but one side of his mask was black and the other was white.

When my eyes finally fell on Will, I was at a loss for words. Somehow the guys had gotten his red hair slicked back, and his mask was a dark red with gold designs on it. His suit was crimson red, and he was tugging at the collar of his shirt with his tie already hanging loose around his neck. When he looked at me, his hand immediately dropped from his collar, and his eyes grew so wide I thought they might pop out of his head through his mask.

Then classical music started up from some hidden speakers in the rafters. No one wanted to be the first ones to dance, but after a few seconds, Lily wasn't going to wait any longer. "Oh, mon dieu, Gabriel, come here," she said while grabbing Gabriel by the wrist and dragging him onto the dance floor. Despite his attempt to protest, he started dancing with her, which created a chain reaction. Preston offered to dance with Grace, which was quite entertaining to watch because of their major size difference. Other employees found partners and started dancing as well. One of the maids even managed to drag Simon on to the dance floor. I made a mental note to ask her how she managed that later on.

Just then I noticed that Elizabeth was standing by herself and nervously glancing at me...no, not at me, at Niko. I gently elbowed him in the side. "Looks like you have a fan." I looked over at Elizabeth, and she sheepishly looked away from me. He followed my gaze, smiled at me, and then headed over to ask her to dance.

"Since when did you become a matchmaker?" I spun around to see Will standing behind me with his usual smirk.

"Eh, he just needed a little push in the right direction. He can be pretty dense when it comes to emotions, like a certain someone I know," I said and raised a playfully, accusing eyebrow at him. Then I remembered he couldn't see it through my mask, so I just smirked at him instead.

"Well, may that certain someone have this dance, mi cielo?" He extended his hand to me like a true gentleman.

I giggled a little before responding, "It would be my pleasure." I took his hand, and we walked out onto the dance floor. When my parents were still alive, they would turn on the record player in the living room on the rare occasion that they were home. They would dance with me and Niko for hours, and it was actually tons of fun. That was what they always considered family night with the occasional board game, of course.

To my surprise, Will was actually a really good dancer. It was easy for us to fall in sync with each other, and it felt like I was dancing on air. Will twirled me and then brought me back close to his chest.

"You're actually a pretty good dancer," I whispered as I laid a soft kiss on his cheek under the rim of his mask.

"If I didn't know how to waltz, I wouldn't have made it through the 1800s. I didn't get a chance to say anything when you came in, but you look breathtaking. That dress really brings out the emerald green of your eyes," he said, pulling me a little closer to him.

"Thank you. You clean up pretty nice too, but I gotta say, I'm not a big fan of the slicked-back hair," I reached up and ruffled his hair until it was sticking out all over the place again. I smiled at him and playfully tilted my head. "Much better." Will laughed at me and then continued dancing.

Throughout the night, I ended up dancing with every one of the major seven and even with my brother for a little while. When the song ended, I stumbled over to the table where Will was sitting and flopped down in one of the chairs, most unladylike, before anyone had a chance to drag me into the next song. I had worn heels before but never to dance in. My feet were killing me, and my legs felt like Jell-O.

"You look like you could use a drink," Will said and held out a champagne glass to me. "Now make sure you don't—"

Before he could finish his warning, I grabbed the glass out of his hand and downed it in one gulp. I immediately regretted it because it burned all the way down and my eyes started watering like crazy. "Holy hell! That burns!" I said while pinching the bridge of my nose and smacking my fist against the table.

Will burst into tears because he was laughing so hard. "I tried to warn ya. The strongest thing you've had is a few drinks of my beer earlier, and you literally just downed an entire glass of champagne. I don't even do that. Stay right here, I'll go get you some water." True to his word, he got me a glass of water, but I was still super leery and decided it would be a good idea to take sips out of the glass until it was empty.

He filled up my glass with water again before I spoke, "Okay, now that I'm not dying, the taste isn't that great either. The beer was definitely better." My throat still stung a little, but it was ten times better than before.

"Yeah, I've always been more partial to beer or hard liquor every once in a while. Wine and champagne were never my strong suit. I'm not a big fan of the fruity stuff." He was still smiling in amusement, but at least he wasn't laughing at me anymore.

"So, I've been meaning to ask, what are the others' languages? I mean, I know that yours is Spanish, Lily's is French, and Gabriel's is Latin, but that's all I know," I said and took another sip of my water.

Will took a long drink of his champagne as if buying himself time to ponder the question before answering me, "Well, the others don't usually use their languages unless they need to activate their weapons, but Elizabeth uses Arabic, Simon uses Greek, Preston uses German, and Grace uses Japanese. We're all fluent in our weapon's language, but we decided it would be easier if we all just learned English. What about your brother? How'd he become so famous at such a young age?"

"I really don't know. He always loved taking pictures, and when he decided he wanted to get away from the supernatural stuff as fast as humanly possible, being a photographer was something he was good at, and he enjoyed it. End of story," I said as a song ended. Then I noticed a strange sound coming from one of the windows. It was very quiet, but it sounded like a tiny alarm beeping. "Will, do you hear that?" I didn't wait for him to answer; I just got up and walked toward the window.

Will followed close behind me until we were only about seven feet from the window, then he grabbed my wrist and yanked me in the other direction. He shouted at the top of his lungs, "Everyone get away from the—"

He only had enough time to pull me close to his chest and turn his back to the window before he was interrupted by a giant explosion. The force of the explosion blew me and Will off our feet and across the floor. This time he was cradling my head in his hand to make sure I was as safe as I could get. My ears were ringing like crazy, but I knew that we couldn't just lay there. I went to push us off of the ground and noticed a pool of blood beneath us. I looked at myself, and I wasn't bleeding anywhere, but that could only mean one thing.

"Oh my gods, Will!"

He was still holding me as tight as he could, but his eyes looked like he was staring at nothing. It was like he was in shock and couldn't untense his grip around me. I couldn't move my arms to smack him, and yelling at him didn't appear to do anything, so I did the only thing I could think to do.

"Gabriel! Lily! Somebody help! Will is hurt!" At first, I couldn't see anyone through all the smoke and dust. Soon a dark figure came through the smoke, but the face I saw couldn't have been real. "Mom?"

CHAPTER 17

Deseat And Liam

My eyes had to be deceiving me. My mother was standing there smiling at me. "Hi, sweetheart. I missed you so much," she said as she walked toward where Will and I were lying on the floor. Her appearance, her voice, even the way she walked was unmistakable.

"Mom...but you...how can you...they said you and Dad were...dead," I stammered out as hot tears forced themselves from my eyes. The tears were a mix of relief, adrenaline, and confusion.

"Ssshh, Paige I'm here now. Don't cry," she said and reached out toward me.

Then Will stirred ever so slightly. "Stay away from her. She's not real, mi cielo. She's a fake." His voice was hoarse, and his arms trembled as he tried to push himself off me, but he still managed to get us both to our feet.

My mother stepped a little closer but dropped her outstretched hand. "Paige, honey, it's me. Would you really believe this stranger over your own mother?" Her betrayed expression was breaking my heart, but what if Will was right? How could I choose between my mother and the man I love? Will wouldn't lie to me, would he? There was only one way I knew for sure to find out.

I took a few steps toward my mother, still holding Will's hand for comfort and as a way to keep myself grounded. "Mom...what was the last thing I said to you?"

"Well, that you love me of course," she said with nervous laughter.

"Oh, Mom…," I said, taking a few more steps toward her. Then in one fluid motion, I dropped Will's hand, grabbed my hairpin out of my messed-up braid, and plunged it into "my mother's" stomach.

She fell to her knees, and a stream of crimson trickled out of the corner of her mouth. "Paige, how could you? How could you do this to me?"

More tears spilled from my eyes, but they weren't tears of sadness or relief—they were tears of rage. "Listen up, you piece of crap, if you wanted to impersonate my mother, you should have done more research. If you were my real mother, you would've known that the last thing I said to you was that I hated you, but there's no way you could have known because the only person I ever told about that is the person standing right behind me. So you can get rid of my mother's face and go straight to hell." I stepped backward until my hand found Will's again. Just that small amount of contact was reassuring.

The thing that looked like my mom let out a horribly amused laugh that sent a shiver down my spine. "You are a lot more perceptive than I thought," it said as it stood up and wiped the blood from its lip. When it yanked the pin out of its stomach and tossed it aside, its body rippled and changed into an all-too-familiar face. Only a few feet from us was Deseat's red hair and wickedly evil smile. No wonder she was called Deseat, she could impersonate whoever she wanted, but she wasn't my main concern at the moment.

I made sure to keep an eye on Deseat while speaking to Will. "Will, how bad are you hurt?"

"I have a pretty large gash across my back, but it should heal quickly. She ruined my perfectly good suit though," he said with a chuckle. His usual cocky sarcasm reassured me that he wasn't hurt too badly, and I let out a sigh of relief. "Where'd you get that hairpin anyway?"

"It was a birthday gift from my brother. I never thought I'd say this, but I guess Niko's protective brother complex can come in handy sometimes." We both laughed at that.

"Remind me to thank him later," Will said and gave my hand a comforting squeeze.

Then I heard Niko's voice through the dust. "Paige, where are you?" Speak of the devil, and he shall come.

"Over here, Niko!" I yelled as the dust finally began to settle. I could see the others standing around the ballroom with their weapons drawn. There were lesser sins and godly monsters scattered around the floor, either unconscious or injured, but none were fatally wounded. The ones that were still standing cautiously made their way behind Deseat.

Niko came running up to me with a concerned look on his face. "Paige, are you all right? Why are you crying? Why are you covered in blood?"

"I'm fine, Niko. It's not my blood, but Will is hurt," I said to reassure him and then turned to face Deseat. I was fed up with all the fighting, and as much as I didn't want to leave Will or any of the other sins, I knew I had to end this case and end it now. "Now do you see what all of your violence has caused? The people who trusted and followed you are now lying on the floor in pain, and for what? For a title? The seven deadly sins are only labeled so on paper. You want their position, but what will that get you? Nothing. They have never treated you any differently because they're just like you, and say you did kill them and get their titles, then what? Someone else will just challenge you for them. Maybe in a hundred years, maybe in a thousand, but someone will kill you for that title just like you're trying to do now. So let me ask you, is a name really worth your life and the lives of the people who trust you?"

Deseat just stared at me with realization dawning on her face, but she was too shocked to speak. Then I felt a hand on my shoulder and turned to see Lily looking at me with tears in her eyes. "Well said, mon cheri." Her hair was disheveled, her dress was torn and dirty, and her makeup was a disaster, but she was giving me the most genuine heartwarming smile I had ever seen. I looked at the others, and even though their appearances were in similar states, they were smiling at me as well. Even though I was so happy I thought that I was going to start crying again, I turned back to Deseat to await her answer.

When she finally spoke, it was with a stammer. "You...you called us people. We've never been considered...people by anyone before."

72

Her response wasn't what I was expecting. "Every single one of us in this room is a person in their own right. It doesn't matter if you're a human, a godly monster, a sin, or even a god, you're still a person because your differences are what make you a person. If you realize that what you're doing is wrong and end your rebellion peacefully, I can talk to my superiors and maybe let you off with just property damage and hospital costs instead of SAHRA prison time."

There was hesitation throughout the entire group, but one boy stepped past Deseat and right up to me. He had short dark brown hair, bright blue eyes, and an innocent smile. He looked like he couldn't be much older than fifteen, but if there was anything I'd learned, it's that things aren't always as they seem.

"I'm Liam Stirling. I'm the sin of Lies, and I personally accept your proposition. This has all gone way too far, and I just want it to be over," he said, then glanced back at Deseat. "Destiny, you know she's right."

Wait, Deseat's human name is Destiny? That's actually a nice name.

Destiny finally stepped forward to stand next to Liam, and I let go of Will's hand to step up and meet them. Just as I extended my hand to shake theirs, the floor beneath me cracked and gave way. The explosion must have weakened the floor because it crumbled under Liam and Destiny as well. "Paige!" I could hear Will shouting my name just before the darkness enveloped me.

CHAPTER 18

Maybe Not So Bad

Next thing I knew, someone was gently tapping the side of my face. "Hey, lady, can you hear me?" It sounded like Liam, but I wasn't sure. With a sudden jolt of pain up my left arm, my mind pulled itself to the surface, and my eyes flew open. Liam and Destiny were leaning over me, and I thought I could make out concerned expressions on their faces through the dark. "Oh, thank the gods you're awake. Hang on, we're going to find a way to get you free," Liam said with a sigh of relief.

What did he mean they were going to get me free? Another jolt of pain made me look over at my left arm, but I couldn't see it. My arm was buried in rubble all the way up to my shoulder. My first instinct was to panic, but I stopped myself because panicking wasn't going to help anyone. In an attempt to take my mind off my throbbing arm, I tried to examine our surroundings. It was kind of hard to tell because the only source of light was the flashlight from Destiny's phone, but it looked like we were in an underground tunnel.

"Where are we?" I asked, my voice hoarse from inhaling so much dust.

As Destiny tried to push some of the bigger boulders off my arm, Liam acknowledged my question. "I'm not exactly sure. We fell through the floor of the mansion, but this doesn't look like a basement, and it felt like we fell longer than that. Um, miss, are you hurt anywhere other than your arm?"

74

THE SINS WITH KIND FACES

I did a mental check of my body but didn't feel major pain anywhere else. "A few bumps and bruises but nothing serious, and my name is Paige. Are either of you hurt?"

"Like you said, a few bumps and bruises but nothing serious. You should be more worried about yourself," he said. Then Destiny pushed another boulder aside, which shifted something in my arm, and I couldn't hold in a cry of pain.

She immediately pulled her hands away from the rubble. "I'm sorry."

"No, you're fine. Just get my arm free, please," I said through clenched teeth, and after a moment of hesitation, she went back to digging. Then I turned back to Liam. "Can you distract me so maybe it won't hurt so bad?"

He looked a little unsure. "Uh…I can try." He moved over to my right side and sat down on a boulder, so I wasn't watching Destiny unbury my arm, which I was thankful for. "What do you want me to do?"

"Well, there's not a lot I can do except talk, but that's okay because I have a lot of questions. Are we the only ones down here? Is there a way out? How long was I unconscious? Why didn't you guys just leave me here?" I asked. I wasn't sure I wanted to dive into the more personal questions just yet, and I needed to know more about our current situation first.

"Um…as far as I know, no one else was close enough to the hole to fall in, and we haven't seen anyone else. We haven't ventured around in these tunnels, but they have to lead somewhere, right? I don't know how long we've been down here all together, but after we woke up, you were only out for a few minutes. As for your last question…we're not heartless. We couldn't just leave you here to die. Besides, you're our only ticket out of prison," he said with a wounded expression.

I remembered Niko saying something about there being catacombs under the mansion when he first moved here. That must be where we were.

"I didn't mean to offend you. You both seem like good people—" I cut my sentence short with a sharp inhale to hold back a yelp. With my line of work, I had had some pretty nasty injuries before, but I was fairly certain that my arm was broken in at least two places and my shoulder was dislocated. "So…I thought that all sins changed their human forms every once in a while to stay under the radar, but why don't they change all the time like Destiny?"

"I don't know where to start with that question…Well, the major seven have weapons, but the rest of us have physical or mental powers. Destiny can take on someone else's image as long as she has had time to study their appearance, but all other sins can only phase to a different form once in a great while because it is extremely painful and draining for us. That's how she could easily conjure up those claws when you first met her…and she studied as much information about your mother as she could find," he said with a guilty expression. Just the thought of her using my mother's face to get close to me made me cringe.

I desperately wanted to change the subject. "Um…I hope you don't mind me asking, but what is your power?"

It was difficult to tell in the dim lighting, but it looked like Liam's face turned red at my question. "Well, it's not very useful, especially not in combat, but I can see heat signatures within sixty feet of where I'm standing. I can turn it off, but when it's active, my eyes glow." With a sheepish smile his eyes, which were already an unnaturally bright blue, started to glow. They were such a beautiful blue that I couldn't resist the urge to smile back at him.

My thoughts were interrupted by Destiny's trembling voice. "Oh…my gods." I looked over to where she had been working to see that she had removed most of the rubble, but I could also see the massive pool of blood around my arm. I wanted to lift my arm and examine the extent of the damage, but I couldn't, which just proved the theory of my shoulder being dislocated. I didn't want to move because it was just going to make the pain even worse, and I didn't know how much more I could take. Destiny's shock must have worn off because she started speaking again. "What should we do?"

That was a really good question. This is what I get for skipping out on most of my first aid classes. "Uh…well, as painful as it's going to be, one of you is going to have to push my shoulder back into the socket. Then we're going to have to find the source of the bleeding, stop it or slow it down, and make a sling out of something so we can find a way out of here," I said, starting to feel kind of light headed, probably from the blood loss.

They glanced at each other with knowing looks, and Liam got up from his rock to walk over to Destiny. Both of them stuck out one of their fists, and I was trying to figure out what they were doing when they answered that question for me. They were chanting, "Rock, paper, scissors, shoe!" Destiny chose rock, and Liam chose paper. They were literally playing rock, paper, scissors to see which one of them was going to push my joints back together!

Destiny rolled her eyes and walked over to my shoulder. Liam turned my face away from it and started speaking to me, "We can use my jacket as a sling, but we're going to need something else to stop the bleeding." He then tugged off his black jacket to use as a sling after we could figure out how to stop the bleeding.

"Well, you can tear strips of material off of the bottom of my dress—" *Crack!* "Aaarrrgghhh!" My scream bounced off the walls and echoed down the tunnel, but I could move my arm again. I lifted my arm and noticed a shimmering white piece of bone sticking out of my forearm. After I gave him permission, Liam started tearing strips of cloth off the skirt of my dress. I was very glad that the girls picked out a dress with a really long skirt.

Liam tied one strip of cloth as tightly as he could right below my shoulder in an attempt to slow down the bleeding, but he wrapped the rest of them around the wound on my arm before tying his jacket around my neck in a makeshift sling. I pulled off my heels and very shakily got to my feet.

"Liam, can you see anything with your heat vision?" I was certain that we needed to find a way out and fast, or I was going to bleed to death. The bone must have punctured a major artery in my arm or something.

Liam's eyes once again turned bright blue as he slowly spun in a full circle. "Maybe a few rats, but nothing that can help us," he said with a defeated expression. I glanced back at where I was buried and realized the cave-in had blocked off the tunnel in that direction, so there was only one way to go, and that was forward.

We started walking, but only got so far before the tunnel split into two different directions, and both options looked like endless black voids. I leaned against the wall with a shiver. It was getting harder and harder to walk. Besides, I had already bled through the cloth and Liam's jacket. Destiny pressed the back of her hand against my forehead and grimaced. "Liam, she's running a fever, and she has lost too much blood. We need to find a way out of here, or she's going to be a goner."

The genuine concern in their expressions was slightly comforting. Just then I remembered a trick that my grandfather taught me to use when I wasn't sure where to go. I stumbled over to the left tunnel and took a deep breath, and it smelled like dirt and dust, then I did the same to the right tunnel. It smelled like rain and the faintest hint of grass. "It's this way," I said before leaning against the wall again.

They both gave me skeptical looks before agreeing. With both of them helping me support my weight, we gradually made our way through the tunnels, stopping at the forks to decide which way to go. We eventually started hearing the rain, which meant we were getting close to the way out.

I began to see the gray moonlight shining ahead of us, and I was relieved because Destiny and Liam were practically dragging me at that point. As we walked out of the tunnel into the moonlight, I could feel the cool raindrops falling on my face. The tunnel opened up to a beautiful little pond with weeping willows all around, and despite the rain, I could hear frogs croaking in the distance.

"We made it, Paige! We're out!" Liam shouted with pure joy. I wanted to share his excitement, but I was so weak from the blood loss that I just collapsed. "No, no, no. Paige, come on, you can't die now," he said as we slid all the way to the ground.

We didn't even know where we were, so there was no way they could get me to a hospital in time. I was going to die. What a crappy twenty-first birthday gift. I wasn't going to be able to keep my promise that Niko wouldn't lose the last family member he had. Will was going to lose me, and right after he had told me how he really felt. I had made so many great friends in the last week, and now I was going to die of blood loss.

"Hello? Is anyone out there!" Now I was hearing Will's voice. I guess that's what happens when you're about to die—hearing the voices of the people you love.

Then Destiny started shouting right next to me, "Over here! Somebody please help us!"

Then I noticed by some miracle that Will's voice wasn't in my head. There were flashlights shining through the trees, and a second later, I could see a group of people running toward us.

Gabriel kneeled down beside me on my left, and Will gently pulled my head onto his lap. Gabriel was moving my arm around to examine it, but as painful as it was, I couldn't find the strength to care. It was starting to become a chore to just keep my eyes open.

Will laced his fingers with mine and gently ran his hand over my head. "Hold on, mi cielo. We're here. Everything is going to be all right." I mustered up all the strength I could to lightly squeeze his hand back. "Gabriel, what's the diagnosis?" I know he was trying to stay positive in front of me, but the fear in his voice clearly showed through.

"Her arm is broken in multiple places, and she's lost way too much blood from the lacerations in her arm. She isn't going to make it half an hour to a hospital, and I don't have any of the necessary tools to perform a blood transfusion at the mansion," he said as he wrapped something else around my arm, but at this point, it was useless.

Then another figure came running toward us, and it took me a second to figure out that it was Niko. His soft and pretty face was drawn tight with worry like I'd never seen before. "I just called SAHRA, and they said that they could be here with medical supplies and an ambulance in ten minutes!" he said, his voice shaking with a mix of fear and concern.

Then Gabriel mumbled, "I don't know if she'll make it that long."

"She'll make it. She has to," Will said as he picked me up into his arms. I could hear his heartbeat racing inside his chest, his warmth a stark contrast to the cold I felt enveloping my body. I couldn't tell whether his words were for my benefit or his own.

We weren't that far from the mansion, but Will made sure not to jostle me as much as possible. Every time my eyes would start to slide shut, he would say something or gently shake me to make sure I stayed awake. We got back, and Will sat down on the outside steps, cradling me close to his chest. He kept repeating, "Everything's going to be okay," but I think he was telling himself that more than me.

My consciousness faded in and out for what felt like hours before I saw the red-and-blue flashing lights along with the sound of the SAHRA siren.

Will practically jumped off the steps and ran me over to the ambulance. I could feel his reluctance to let me go when the paramedics took me out of his arms and laid me down on something soft in the back of the ambulance. I heard the familiar rev of Will's motorcycle before they shut the doors. The paramedics were saying a bunch of medical stuff that I didn't understand, but Alex was beside me the whole time, holding my hand and telling me that everything was going to be all right. I don't know if it was caused by the blood loss, sedatives, or a bit of both, but I quickly lost consciousness.

CHAPTER 19

Case Conclusion and Confession

When I came to, I was in one of the infirmary rooms at HQ. I felt super weak and dizzy, but they must've had me on enough painkillers to keep my arm from throbbing. Then over the stench of rubbing alcohol and latex, I caught the familiar scent of Will's cologne. He had fallen asleep in a chair next to me with his hand around mine and his head lying on my bed. He must have been with me since I arrived because there were dark circles under his eyes, red stubble had started to show on his face, and he was still wearing his suit, minus the jacket and tie. His shirt was torn down the back, but there was no other evidence of a wound ever being there.

My left arm was casted at a right angle all the way up to slightly below my shoulder. I knew that I should probably notify a doctor that I was awake, but I didn't want to disturb Will. He looked so peaceful when he slept, and he also looked like he could use it too. Just then the door to my room opened, and Niko walked in with a cup of coffee in each hand. His face lit up when he saw that I was awake, but I shushed him before he had time to freak out and wake up Will in the process. He had dark circles under his eyes too, but at least he had changed his clothes and shaved.

He put the Styrofoam cups on a small table at the head of my bed and very carefully leaned over to hug me like he needed to make sure that I was really there. "You scared the ever living out of me, sis," he whispered, his raspy voice proving that he hadn't slept. He pulled away and smiled. "How are you feeling?"

I groaned. "Like every muscle in my body has gone on vacation and put up their Do Not Disturb signs. I haven't felt this weak in a long time." Then I noticed a small bandage on his arm. "What happened to your arm?"

He glanced down at the bandage before answering, "That's where they stuck me with the needle. You needed a blood transfusion, and apparently us being twins meant we had the same blood type. They would only let me give so much blood though, so William volunteered as well. His blood type is O negative, so he could donate blood to you as well."

I looked at Will, who was still sound asleep and smiled at him. I turned back to Niko with a sigh. "You should probably tell Alex or one of the nurses that I'm awake. I need to talk to Alex about the case anyway."

Niko gently kissed the top of my head with a smile. "All right, I'll go get him, but you have quite a few visitors sitting out in the hallway. Your doctor didn't want a lot of people in here while you were out, but if you're okay with it now, I'll tell them they can come in."

I nodded before he headed for the door.

Right before he opened it, I called over to him, "Wait. Could you tell them to wait outside for five more minutes? I...I'd like a few moments alone." As I spoke, I instinctively glanced down at Will.

My brother gave a knowing look, said, "Sure," and walked out the door. I wanted to talk to Will alone before who all was out there came barging in. I started shaking his hand that was still protectively holding mine. "Will? Will, wake up."

His eyes slowly fluttered open, and he looked up at me. His sleepy eyes were absolutely adorable, but in a second, his drowsiness was gone, and he wrapped me in a crushingly tight hug. "I'm so glad that you're awake, mi cielo," he said, his voice trembling with relief. When he finally pulled away, he cupped my face in both of his hands. They were warm and gentle. His face was so close to mine that I could see streaks on his cheeks where tears had been. It was hard to believe that Will would cry enough over anything to leave red streaks. "How are you feeling? Should I get a doctor? How long have you been awake?"

"No, no, no. It's okay. Niko went to go get Alex, and I haven't been awake very long. Uh, he told me that you donated blood for me. Thank you," I said while placing my hand over top of his.

"Mi cielo...I'd do anything for you." He finished his passionate statement with a soft yet desperate kiss. I kissed him right back without hesitation. I really did love him more than I had ever loved anyone before, and at that moment, I wanted to stop time so I wouldn't have to leave him.

"Are we interrupting something?" We broke our kiss and looked up to see Gabriel sticking his head in through the door.

Will sighed and said, "Yeah, actually you are."

A mischievous smirk spread across Gabriel's face. "Well, too bad!" He threw open the door and mockingly marched right in, with everyone else following behind him. Before I had time to react, Grace had sprinted to my bedside and wrapped me in a death grip of a hug. Why are all my friends so much stronger than me?

"We thought you were going to die. Don't ever scare us like that again," she said while tightly squeezing my shoulders and staring me right in the eyes. They cared. It made me feel better that there were so many people who were concerned for my well-being.

"What Grace is trying to say, mon cheri, is that we are very glad that you are all right," Lily said with her usual smile. They were all in better shape than Niko and Will, but I thought I could see their muscles relax a little just by being in the room with me.

"Do you know how troublesome you've been? You had everyone thinking you were dead." Simon groaned in dismay. Did he really still think I was just a pain in the neck?

Preston laughed and playfully smacked him on the back. "Come on, man. You were at least a little bit worried about her, and you know it."

Simon looked away with a scoff. "Whatever."

I couldn't hold back a chuckle at their adorable bickering. Then I saw Niko and Alex walk through the door with Destiny and Liam, both in power-canceling cuffs. I tried to push myself into a sitting position, but my efforts were in vain with only being able to use one arm. Thankfully Will noticed my struggling and helped me sit up.

The tiny room was now extremely crowded with the major seven, my brother, my boss, and two lesser sins swarmed around my bed. I was starting to feel a little claustrophobic.

"Um, I know you guys just got in to see me, and I'm happy to see all of you as well, but I need to close my case. If you wouldn't mind, can everyone step outside except for Alex, Destiny, and Liam?"

Will and Niko were about to protest when Lily grabbed them both by the shoulder. "Come now, boys. She is a grown woman and can take care of herself for a little while." She pushed both of them out the door and winked at me before following. The others left as well, but not without showing their hesitation.

"All right Striffe, what is your conclusion of the case and the sentence for these two as well as their followers?" Alex asked, trying to be professional in front of Destiny and Liam, but it was clear that he had been just as worried about me as Niko.

I looked over at them, and they both showed a snowstorm of emotions. Fear, anxiety, drowsiness, and even a pinch of relief were flying around in the whirlwind of tension surrounding them. Destiny and Liam weren't criminals; they just made some mistakes. Hell, most people in their positions would've done the exact same thing, and if it weren't for them, I'd be dead in an underground tunnel. "Alex, it is true that this case is concluded, but only because these two admitted that they were wrong. They agreed to pay for any property damage as well as hospital bills, but they aren't criminals, and if it weren't for them, I would be dead. Remove their chains because they are no longer after the seven deadly sins. That is the end of my case."

Destiny's and Liam's faces lit up with relief as Alex unlocked their cuffs. Liam came over to stand by my bed. "Paige, we can never hope to repay you, and we could never ask you to completely forgive us for what we've done, but if the gods allow it, we may become allies. I will be praying to them for forgiveness and also that your injuries heal soon. Farewell, Paige Striffe." Then he walked out the door with Destiny close behind, but she gave me a small sympathetic wave before leaving.

I sighed and relaxed into the bed. "Alex, hand me one of those cups of coffee before I lose my mind." My mind was still a little fuzzy, and I was friggin' exhausted.

He quickly did as I said and snatched the case documents up off my bed before I had time to even find a pen. "You aren't allowed to do anything else even closely related to work until your wounds are completely healed. Dear gods, Paige, I thought you were as good as dead, and even when you do return to work, you're going to be stuck doing desk work for a month! Maybe even longer than that! You're grandfather trusted me to take care of you, and if you had died, I—"

"Alex!" I shouted at him. "I didn't die. I'm still here, and that's all there is to it. I'll take whatever punishment that will make you feel better, but for the love of the gods, don't lecture me about it. I legitimately thought that I was going to die, so I don't want to hear any more about it."

He was shocked at my outburst, but didn't pursue the subject any further.

After an uncomfortable silence, he spoke up again, "I need to head back to my office, but I'll tell the others that they can come back in. Take care of yourself, kid."

I nodded at him, and he smiled at me before he left.

The second the door shut, it flew right back open, and everybody piled back inside, with Niko and Will leading the charge. "Do you need anything?" they asked me at the same time and then glanced at each other in surprise.

I chuckled before responding, "Well...you could tell me when they intend to let me go home and how I'm going to take care of everyday chores once I do."

Niko beat Will to a response. "They said you can be released in a day or two. If you want to stay at my mansion, my housekeepers can keep an eye on you, but if you insist that you want to go home, then I can try and reschedule my photo shoots so I can help out around your apartment."

"No. I do want to go home, but I couldn't ever ask you to postpone your job so you can look after me for months," I said and took a long drink of my pathetic excuse for a cup of coffee. It tasted more like watered-down dirt than coffee, but it was caffeine, so I didn't really have any room to complain.

"If it wouldn't be an intrusion, then I could stay at your place and help out while you're healing. Your brother wouldn't have to take off work. I don't have anything better to do, and I, William Smith, swear that I will be a perfect gentleman," he said with a mocking butler-like bow. I wanted so badly to smack him on the arm, but I couldn't reach. Curse this stupid cast.

I hadn't really considered that possibility. As much as I hated the idea, I just thought that as soon as the case was over, I would never see Will or any of the other major seven again. I jumped at the opportunity to not have to turn my back on them. "You wouldn't be intruding, and like you implied, it would be better for everyone." It took a little convincing, but everyone finally agreed that Will's idea was the best we had.

After being stuck in that hospital room for another two days, I was finally okayed to go home, and I was ecstatic. I didn't like the infirmary anyway, but when Will came into my room to take me home, I was the happiest person in the world.

"Hello, mi cielo. Are you ready to go?" he asked with his usual cocky smirk.

"I will be as soon as you help me put on this sling to support my cast." I had to have one of the nurses help me put on the clothes that Niko had brought over a few hours before. I hated feeling so helpless, but there was nothing I could do about it. I couldn't keep a wide smile off my face when I thought about spending time with Will.

"It would be my pleasure," he said as he gently slid the sling over my head and around my casted arm. "Lily let me borrow her jeep to take you home because she wouldn't let me drive you around on my motorcycle, which I kind of don't blame her. May I escort you to your vehicle, madame?" He extended his arm for me to take, and I did without hesitation.

CHAPTER 20

Finally Home

Apparently Niko had shown Will where my apartment was and where I kept the spare key, so I was home before I knew it. The familiar sounds and scents of home were more welcoming than ever. Then I heard the unmistakable jingle of a bell before my striped gray tomcat came running out of my room toward me.

I bent down and scratched his head as he rubbed against my legs. "Uno, I missed you too buddy. Did Mr. Henry take good care of you while I was gone?" He looked up at me with his emerald-green eyes and meowed happily.

"Who's Mr. Henry?" Will asked while setting my things from the infirmary on the coffee table in front of my couch.

"He's an old man who also lives on the third floor. He's friends with Alex, so whenever I'm given an overnight case, Alex calls him to take care of Uno while I'm gone. Uno has food and water dispensers, so all he really has to do is clean out the litter box every morning," I said. Then I noticed a box wrapped in beautiful rose wrapping paper and a black bow sitting on my coffee table next to the bear he had won for me at the amusement park and the hairpin Niko had given me, minus the blood. "What's that?"

A smirk spread across his face. "That's your birthday gift from me that you didn't get to open. The others said they wanted to give you their gifts personally."

I sat down on the couch and sloppily tore the wrapping paper off of the box. Then I opened it, and what I pulled out made me laugh. It was a motorcycle helmet with a blue rose vine decal around it and a skull decal on either side. "Thanks, it'll be our little inside joke," I said and got up to stumble to my room. I pushed open the door but looked back at Will. "I would like to talk to you, and you don't have to be afraid of entering my bedroom. I won't tell anyone." I winked at him before heading straight for my bed.

I wanted so badly to jump onto my bed like a child, but I knew that would be very unwise in my condition, so I just sat down on the left side and waited for Will to follow me into my room. He leaned against the doorway with a devilish smirk, but there was a glimmer of skepticism in his eyes. "So what did you want to talk to me about, mi cielo?" he asked while crossing his arms.

I patted the other side of the mattress. "Come lay with me?" He hesitated for a second before coming over to lay on the bed next to me. He wrapped his arm around my shoulders, and I snuggled close to him. I took a deep whiff of his cologne before speaking, "We both know that my case involving your safety is over, but I don't want *us* to be over. You and your siblings were more than just another case to me, and even though you're not the kind of person to be nailed down and my life will be extremely short compared to yours, would you consider…staying with me? Because, Will…I love you."

The silence that followed my confession was painstaking, but he finally pulled me into a kiss that could have been an answer all on its own. Way too soon, he pulled away to look me right in the eyes, and his looked like raging infernos.

"I'm so happy you finally said it because I love you too, mi cielo, and I couldn't imagine spending my life with anyone else." He then kissed my forehead before holding me tight to his chest. "Now close your eyes and get some rest. I'll be right here when you wake up."

I knew that there would be a lot more challenges ahead of me, but I also knew that as long as I had Will, I could overcome any obstacles that were thrown my way. We could take the larger steps of a relationship as they came to us, but I was focused on the there and then, and all I wanted to do was fall asleep in the safety of Will's arms. A warm smile drew across my face as I snuggled a little closer to him, and just before I drifted off to sleep, I mumbled, "William... thank you."

The End
Maybe...

About the Author

This is Oliver R. Cross's first published book. He is currently working on a creative writing degree at Miami University. Oliver goes by they/them or he/him pronouns. He is living with family and his two cats while pursuing his education.

Printed in the USA
CPSIA information can be obtained
at www.ICGtesting.com
LVHW041244051023
760079LV00002B/639